ATONEMENT

LOVE UNDERCOVER, BOOK 3

LK SHAW

Want a **FREE** short story?
What about **FREE** chapters of **FOREVER** delivered to your inbox?

Be sure to sign up for my newsletter and download your copy of A Birthday Spanking, a Doms of Club Eden prequel! You'll also start receiving bi-weekly chapters of the novella Forever

You'll also receive infrequent updates about what I'm working on, alerts for sales and new releases, and other stuff I don't share elsewhere!

Atonement, Love Undercover, Book 3
© 2020 by LK Shaw
Cover design © 2020 by PopKitty Designs
Editor: Dayne Hart, Hart to Heart Editing

❀ Created with Vellum

Doms of Club Eden

Submission

Desire

Redemption

Protect

Betrayal

My Christmas Dom

Absolution

Forever (A prequel) - Coming July 2020

Love Undercover Series

In Too Deep

Striking Distance

Atonement

Other Books

Love Notes: A Dark Romance

SEALs in Love

Say Yes

Black Light: Possession

Saving Evie: A Brotherhood Protectors

CHAPTER 1

Two years ago

LONELINESS GNAWED AT ME. Any friends I had were long gone. Driven away by my self-destruction. Clean-and-sober me tried making new ones, but going to the club, getting drunk, and finding some chick to take home and bang wasn't my thing. Which was why I was sitting in a hotel bar, on a Saturday night, drinking water.

Alone.

I was here, because otherwise, I'd be out *there*. On the streets.

The urge grew stronger every day. I could curb it for a little while, but then it would crash through me again like a tidal wave until I thought I'd drown in want and need. The water was mid-chest level, the pressure mounting. Soon, I'd be suffocating, gasping for air that was there but couldn't fill my lungs. The sensation would overwhelm me, and I'd do what I always did to get rid of it.

Use.

Anything to make me fly high above the ocean of guilt and pain. The self-hatred would, of course, follow once I landed. Then the cycle would begin again.

It had been this way for a decade. Ten long years of leaving destruction in my wake.

Four years was the longest I'd managed to fight. It seemed like eons ago.

I'd talked to my brother today, though we weren't close. Not anymore. Every time we saw each other, he'd say something which would only fuel the never-ending guilt inside me. My defense mechanism was to be an asshole. We'd argue, say hurtful things neither of us could take back, and then we wouldn't talk for months. It was our routine, and one I didn't see changing anytime soon.

"Would you like some more water, sir?" The waitress asked for the third time.

I handed her my glass, and she refilled it before handing it back. She picked up the empty dinner plate in front of me and set the check face-down on the table. "I'll take this whenever you're ready."

"Thanks." I took a long draw of my water, the icy coldness of it almost burning my throat as it descended to settle in my stomach. I smirked at the imaginary sloshing sound it probably made hitting the inside of my gut. My humor always leaned toward the dark side.

My gaze traveled around the room, my leg bouncing in a nervous twitch. The hotel restaurant was slow tonight. Which was surprising for a weekend. A lot of empty tables, and only three people sitting at the bar—four, if I counted the suit-clad businessman, with his smarmy salesman smile looming over a blonde woman. My bobbing limb slowed. Old boy certainly wasn't taking the hint that blondie wasn't interested. In fact, she was as oblivious to his presence as he seemed to be to the fact she was practically collapsing in on herself. He ran his finger down her arm, and she shifted on the bar stool, putting a few inches of distance between them.

I'd never been the savior type. Fuck, I couldn't even save myself. But there was a tightness to her, a rigid energy, that screamed for help. Before I changed my mind, I rose from the corner booth I'd parked myself at and strode toward the couple. I should mind my own business. If the woman wanted the guy to leave she could tell him. But for whatever reason, my feet kept propelling me forward until I stood on the woman's right, close enough she could hear me speak, but far enough away that I didn't invade her personal space. Unlike dickwad.

"Is this guy bothering you?" I asked softly.

The woman flinched and the suit straightened and sent me a withering look, like I was a pile of shit he'd stepped in with his favorite wingtip shoes.

"Who the fuck are you?" He sneered.

I ignored him. Instead, I waited for the woman to answer. Her response was the only one I gave a shit about.

She continued staring down into her almost empty rocks glass, her wavy blonde hair a curtain over the side of her face.

"I just want to be left alone." There was a note of emotion in her tone. One I'd heard more than once in rehab and during the many NA meetings I'd attended over the years from those who'd hit rock bottom. It was the bitter tone of anguish.

I smirked at the suit. "Pretty sure that's your cue. The lady's not interested."

He glared at me before sending her a scathing look and

picked up the drink he'd set on the bar. "Whatever." Then he disappeared with a final curl of his lip.

Not once during the entire interaction had she glanced up at either of us. She'd stayed hidden behind the armor of her hair. Aside from her single sentence to be left alone, she hadn't spoken again. Not even a thank you. Taking her at her word, my presence was also not wanted or needed. I returned to my booth and took another drink, my eyes continuing to dart back to the blonde every so often.

The bartender brought her several more drinks. She sipped each one, her delicate fingers clasping the glass, condensation dripping off the bottom of it. After suit guy left, no one else bothered her. She sat alone, completely lost in her own world. Yet I remained sitting here, watching the woman like some creeper.

There was something about her that kept nudging at me. Some compulsion kept me here. I'd only seen a portion of her face through the cascade of her hair. Her cheekbones appeared sharp enough to cut glass. A pale pink lip-color did nothing to plump up her too thin lips. The tip of her nose curved upward. None of the pieces fit together.

It was her eyes, though, that I hadn't caught a glimpse of.

I'd moved to stand near her, spoke to her, smelled her—a hint of lavender and vanilla—and still she'd remained gazing into her glass as though it held some secret. What was her story?

After a quick glance at my watch, I was shocked that it was nearly nine p.m. *Jesus, how had it gotten so late?* I'd been observing her for over two hours. A time in which my earlier urge had quieted. She'd occupied my entire mind, so it hadn't focused on anything but her. I was reluctant to leave, but I needed to go. I dug out my wallet and threw enough cash on the table to pay the bill plus a tip.

The woman had made it clear she wanted to be left alone, but I wanted to check one last time to make sure she was all right before I headed out. Especially after watching her slam back the rest of yet another drink. A pull from some string drew me over to her.

"Excuse me." I waited a beat to see if she'd finally look at me. She didn't, but I forged ahead. "I'm not trying to bother you, but I wanted to make sure you were okay before I left."

Behind the fall of her hair, her lids drifted shut for a moment before they opened again. She slowly raised her head and stared directly in front of her. No other movement. I took the silence as her answer.

"I hear ya loud and clear. Just…be careful." I pivoted, but her whispered request stopped me in my tracks.

"Don't go."

CHAPTER 2

NINETEEN YEARS ago to the day. I glanced at my watch. Nineteen years, seven hours, twenty-three minutes, and sixteen, seventeen, eighteen seconds to be exact.

Every year I think this time things will be different. Yet every year it has remained the same. I'd spend tomorrow sobering up, and on Monday I'd be back to work for another three-hundred sixty-four days. Until next year's anniversary rolled around. Then I'd spend another entire day trying, and failing, to forget, and the cycle would begin again.

I motioned for the bartender to bring me another drink.

With every breath I took, the scent of spring and sunshine still hovered lightly in the air around me. I wished it would go away. It reminded me of rebirth and new beginnings at a time I was only thinking of death.

The man who'd smelled that way had long disappeared. He'd asked me a question, one that had taken me a minute to process, and the hairs on my arm had stood on end. His voice had been gravelly with a raspy quality that reminded me of that first swallow of bourbon. The one that burns going down, but then settles warmly in your belly.

Ever since he'd run off the other guy, his scent had lingered. With a shudder, I tossed back the rest of my drink and waved for the next. A shift in the air brought with it a stronger whiff of the fragrance I'd been trying to purge from my nose.

"Excuse me." A shiver danced across my skin at that same raspy voice. "I'm not trying to bother you, but I wanted to make sure you were okay before I left."

I closed my eyes. I was the farthest thing from okay. Normally, no one bothered me while I was like this, but it would seem *something* about tonight was different. No, I wasn't okay. But maybe, for a short time, I could forget.

"Don't go."

The stranger paused in his retreat. I still couldn't see him, but I could feel him. His body heat anyway, even though he was several steps away. And I could most definitely smell him. Especially after he sat on the bar stool next to me.

"I'm Preston." He didn't offer to shake my hand. Just those two words spoken softly. His bourbon-smooth voice washed over me. I didn't know what it was about him, maybe a quiet strength, but I wanted to keep him talking. Inhaling some courage, I swiveled in my seat and met hazel eyes surrounded by long lashes. An echo of my own pain ricocheted inside them.

"Sara." The name spilled from my lips before I could call it back. Then I didn't want to.

Preston's expression shifted, and he drew back a little. "It's nice to meet you, Sara."

I ignored the change in his demeanor. "It's nice to meet

you as well. I didn't say thank you earlier. You know, for running that guy off."

"No problem." He paused for a moment. "You seemed to be having a bad night."

I let out a humorless sound. "What makes you think I'm having a bad night?"

He shrugged noncommittally. My eyes traveled over him, and the sight of something on his arms made me pause. On the right, from the wrist all the way up until it disappeared under his shirt sleeve, was black tribal ink. That wasn't what caught my attention. The area surrounding the bend in his elbow had. It was devoid of color. Present, though, were small, pinkish, circular raised scars dotted randomly along the skin. A glance at his left inner arm showed similar markings. I met his gaze. Preston's face was blank.

"Are those...?" I don't know why I bothered asking. I worked for the D.E.A. I knew what track marks looked like.

He nodded. "Been clean almost a year."

"I'm surprised you don't try to hide them." Ouch. That had come across awfully holier-than-thou. Who was I to judge anyone?

Preston turned his arms over, fully exposing them. "Hiding them doesn't erase what I've done, so why bother? They remind me of who I used to be, who I am, and who I want to become. I forget sometimes."

"Who did you used to be?"

His lips barely curled in the slight resemblance of a smile. "A son. A brother. But I was never really any good at being either of those."

A daughter. That's who I used to be. "Who do you want

to become?" I asked softly, leaning closer, almost desperate to hear his response.

Preston's hazel eyes met mine, and I held my breath. Inside them was pain. The kind that resonated with the sharp blade of agony I lived with on a daily basis.

"Someone who's worthy of atonement for my sins."

I sucked in the breath I'd been holding. "How will you know you're worthy?"

"When I've forgiven myself."

A lump formed in my throat, and I swallowed it down. "I have sins to forgive myself for, too," I choked out.

What possessed me to say that? I'd never told a soul what I'd done. It was my deepest, darkest secret. One I'd lived with for nineteen years.

Warmth covered my hand, and I looked down to see Preston had laid his on top of mine. He gave it a tiny, comforting squeeze. Our eyes met.

"You will. One day." That's all he said. He didn't ask what I'd done that needed forgiving. Only said that, some day, forgiveness would happen. His beautiful, hazel eyes fixed on mine as though willing me to believe him. To have faith.

His thumb skated along my cheek, and wetness smeared across my skin. *Was I crying?* I hadn't cried since that long ago day. Not once.

I almost hated this stranger for dragging out emotions I kept buried. At the same time, I wanted to purge them completely. This lonely existence was slowly killing me. There was no one in my life. No family. No real friends. Yet, the moment I locked eyes with this man, it was like he understood all the pain inside me. Like he suffered too.

Did I dare to hope, if only for a night, that I could

unburden this crushing weight onto someone stronger? Would I wake up in the morning and drown in regret? Probably. At the moment, though, I didn't care.

I covered Preston's hand and leaned into his caress. His fingers were thick and strong. With the barest movement, my lips brushed his palm. His callouses were rough. Visions of him touching the rest of my body sent a throbbing heaviness to my core.

Preston's eyes darkened with arousal as I stared up at him. My tongue darted out to wet my lips, and his gaze dropped to lock onto them. Seeing how affected he was gave me courage.

"Would you like to come up to my room?"

CHAPTER 3

Present day

"Why did you let him talk you into this?" I grumbled under my breath as I sat in my parked car outside a cute ranch-style house in a quiet neighborhood in the northwest suburbs of Chicago. Being here was a mistake. I hadn't wanted to come in the first place, but Brody was a…friend, and he'd asked nicely. Still, I should go home, call and tell him something came up, and apologize for missing the party.

I rested my forehead against the steering wheel. God, I was such a coward. All I had to do was go in there, say my hellos, drop off my gift, and then leave. Easy enough. I didn't have to make conversation. I barely knew these people. Yes, I'd helped Brody's future brother-in-law, Victor, rescue his girlfriend after she'd been kidnapped, but that had been a month ago. I hadn't talked to or seen any of them since then.

"Shit."

I grabbed the bottle of wine and jumped out of my car before I could change my mind. My lungs burned from the burst of cold air that hit them. My breath came out on a plume of smoke. My feet were like hundred pound weights being dragged up the sidewalk. I paused at the door, nowhere near ready to face who might be inside. Fuck this. My fingers were already feeling numb from the cold, so I rang the bell.

It opened to a lovely young Latina woman smiling at me. She glowed, and I couldn't help glancing down at her slightly curved belly.

"Landon, I'm so glad you came." Ines, Brody's girlfriend, welcomed me inside.

"Here, this is for you guys." I cringed as she took my offering. Who gives a pregnant woman a bottle of wine?

"You didn't have to bring anything but thank you. I'll be ready to crack this thing open by the time this kid gets here, I'm sure. You can hang your coat on the rack there. Brody will be happy to see you."

Reluctantly, I shrugged out of the garment. I didn't want to be here long enough to hang it up. I was glad the two of them were back in Chicago, safe, happy, and in love, but housewarming parties and being surrounded by this large, boisterous family wasn't my thing. Being in close quarters near this many people made me twitchy. It reminded me of everything I'd had at one time, but lost.

"Everyone's in here. Can I get you a drink?" she asked over her shoulder.

I cleared my throat. "No, thanks. I'm good. I can't stay long."

I followed her into the living room, my stomach twisting in knots and my heartbeat thumping in my ears. As though some force of nature commanded it, my gaze shifted to the far wall, and I found myself staring into familiar hazel eyes. My steps faltered.

Memories blasted through me. Sweat-slicked skin. Whispered promises. The bittersweet agony of thinking my sins could be forgiven.

I shoved the unwelcome thoughts away and focused my gaze on the three people standing in front of me. Brody, holding a red plastic cup in his hand, Ines, and her father.

"You came." My former agent sounded surprised. He reached out and awkwardly one-arm hugged me.

Sweat covered my palms, and my stomach dipped. I forced a smile, but it was a weak one. "I figured the least I could do was formally welcome you back."

"Well, I'm glad you're here. You remember Ernesto?" he indicated the older man standing next to him.

I nodded. "It's a pleasure to see you again, Mr. Rodriguez."

Before I could guess his intent, he wrapped his arms around me for a quick hug. I tried not to flinch. I wasn't a hugger, and I'd just been given two. He pulled back and smiled widely at me, his teeth bright white against the darker tone of his skin. "Please, call me Ernesto. Thank you for helping my son and Estelle."

Uncomfortable with his gratitude, I took a tiny step back. "You're welcome."

Ines gestured to the crowded room. "I think you know everyone here, except for Manuel's wife, Marguerite, and their two kids."

Avoiding looking at the man on the other side of the room, I took in the rest of the Ines' family. Her brother Victor and his girlfriend, Estelle, cuddled on the couch. Her other two brothers, and a woman who must be the sister-in-law, stood in the kitchen. A couple of young children, a dark-haired girl and boy, raced past us, giggling and laughing.

"Oh, wait, you don't know Brody's brother. Let me introduce you."

"No!" All three blinked at my tone. "I mean, we met outside that warehouse a month ago."

Ines' expression cleared first. "That's right, he was there."

And I'd avoided him like the fucking plague until I could slip away with my two colleagues. I'd felt his gaze following me the whole time. The same way I could feel eyes boring into my back today. Coming here was a bad idea.

Conversation flowed around us. People moved in and out of the room. Time passed far too slowly, and my eyes kept darting toward the door. I didn't know what time it was, but surely I'd been here long enough that it wouldn't be rude if I grabbed my coat and said my goodbyes? Especially since he was here. Once again, flashes of memories pierced my brain. That had been the most beautiful, and one of the most painful, nights of my life.

My hollow laughter joined everyone else's, even though I had no idea what I was laughing at. I needed to get out of here. Now. "Thank you for inviting me to the party, but I have to run. I'm glad you're back, Brody."

I barely waited for a response before hightailing it out of the house, pulling my coat up around my ears. I couldn't remember the last time it had been this cold this early, but that was Chicago for you.

I reached my car, and the voice that hadn't left my head for two years, the one I could pick out blindfolded, hit my ears. "Leaving so soon?"

It was far too close for comfort. I froze and quickly tried

to make my escape, but the second I tugged on the handle, a strong hand slammed across the top of my car door, halting its movement.

"Move your hand," I bit out behind clenched teeth.

My gaze locked on the fingers in front of me. They looked exactly the same as they had before. Calloused. Strong. Gentle. A brief flash of them cupping my breast, thumbing my nipple, rushed through my mind. I pushed the images away, needing to get out of here.

Hating him for making me look at him, I raised my eyes to meet hazel ones. It almost hurt to see Preston's face again. His expression echoed the pain I forced down. He took a tiny step back. Not far enough away, because if I wanted, I could still reach out and touch him.

"Why'd you run?"

I closed my eyes, needing to break this connection. I also needed to block out my emotions. He'd seen too much of them already.

Hoping my mask was back in place, I met his stare again. "I didn't *run*. I left. We had a good time, and it was over."

Preston crossed his arms. "Liar."

I flinched. Even after two years, he still saw too much.

"You and I both know it was more than just a good time, Landon."

Hearing that name from his lips hardened my emotions. He met Sara that night. I needed to put a stop to this. Pushing back my shoulders, I straightened to my full height. "We fucked. That was it. Nothing more, nothing less."

"Does Brody know?"

I reared back. "God, no. I didn't even know he was your brother until that day outside the warehouse. He'd told me he had a recovering addict brother, but no fucking way could I have guessed it was you."

"I've never forgotten you," he said softly.

Pain shot through me. I'd never forgotten him, either, no matter how hard I tried. But he was no good for me. He made me feel things I didn't deserve to feel.

It was time to end this conversation. I glared hard at him, desperate to show how much I didn't care. "It was two years ago. You should get over it. I know I have."

I grabbed the handle hard again, and yanked the door open, knocking Preston out of the way. I dove behind the wheel, and with barely a glance for other cars, I took off down the street, refusing to look in the rearview mirror to see if he was still standing there.

Why now? Why did he have to show up in my life again? I'd purged him from my system. I *had*, damn it.

I made it home. I tried opening the front door, but my hand shook so much I couldn't get the key in the lock. I took a deep breath to steady myself, and finally, after two more tries I got it open. I dropped my things on the side table next to the door and shrugged out of my coat, just as a large bundle of orange fluff came bounding into the room. With a purr as loud as a diesel engine, my tabby, Sherbert, snaked around my legs, leaving a trail of cat hair behind.

I picked him up and cuddled him, needing the closeness of his rumbling vibration to cheer me up. He chirped in my ear.

"I missed you too." With a kiss on his nose, I set him down and made my way to the kitchen.

I flopped on the couch and took a sip of the beer I'd grabbed. Sherbert jumped onto my lap and curled up to sleep. I envied the big guy. Absently, I stroked his fur as memories from inside that hotel room played in my head. Whispered words of pleasure. Feeling more connected to another human being than I ever had. Looking into Preston's eyes had, for a brief time, quieted the riotous screams of agony that seemed to always be present inside my head.

It had been one of the rare times the nightmares hadn't visited me. As though his presence alone scared them away. They returned though.

They always did.

I jumped off the couch, dumping the cat on the floor with an aggrieved howl, and stood shaking.

I cursed Preston Thomas for showing back up in my life and dragging out things best left buried.

A quick glance at the clock showed it was still early afternoon. Maybe she'd be in her office. I grabbed the phone and dialed the number I knew by heart, because I called her far too often.

"Hey, Doc, I know it's late notice, but do you think you can fit me in today?" I let out a heavy sigh. "It's been a rough one."

CHAPTER 4

"About time you dragged your sorry ass in here."

Brody took a pull from his paper coffee cup and shot me the finger as he closed the office door with his foot. "Fuck off. I'm only ten,"—he paused at my throat clearing and corrected himself. "Fine, I'm twenty minutes late. It's not like we have clients banging down the door."

Thomas Brothers: Private Investigators had been open for business approximately twenty minutes, and the least qualified brother had arrived first.

"Not only are you late, but you didn't even have the decency to bring me a cup of coffee with you."

My brother narrowed his eyes. "You don't drink coffee."

I shrugged. "It still would have been a nice gesture."

"Good god. You're not going to be like this every day, are you?" Brody grumbled as he plopped into the office chair that groaned under his weight. I smirked and waited for it to collapse beneath him. Would serve him right for buying hand-me-down furniture from a consignment store. If he'd waited, I could have scored us higher quality products for a better deal. It would have been stolen merchandise, but Brody didn't need to know that. Too late now.

"Are you regretting asking me to be your business partner already?"

"I only walked through the door five minutes ago. Give me at least an hour, and I'll let you know."

I blew out a puff of air. "Man, who would have thought you and I would be working together one day?"

The idea still blew me away. Brody tried leaning back in his chair. He sat upright after it let out a rumble of protest in response.

"Well, technically I'm the boss since I *am* the one who put up eighty percent of the capital for this little business venture."

"I guess that means you *technically*,"—I emphasized with air quotes—"get to do most of the work then, right? I'll sit here and do all this filing." My hands waved over the empty surface of my desk.

"You really are going to be a pain in my ass, aren't you?" He took another sip from his cup, and I couldn't hold back my smile.

It felt good to bust each other's balls. For so long we'd had a tenuous relationship. It was still by no means perfect, but over the last year we'd worked hard on repairing it. My continued sobriety helped.

"How's Ines doing? Are you two going to find out the sex of the baby?" I couldn't believe I was going to be an uncle.

"We can't agree. I want to be surprised, but she wants to know. She has her next ultrasound appointment in a few weeks, and she should be far enough along to tell by then."

"Whatever it ends up being, he or she will be one lucky

kid to have you two as parents." I was almost envious of this baby, and he hadn't even been born yet.

"You really think so?"

I was surprised by the nervousness in my brother's question. "Without a doubt. You were the best big brother a guy could ask for, so I have no doubt you'll be the best dad as well."

Brody looked thoughtful for a moment, and then he blinked before catching my eye. "I don't know. Maybe if I'd been a better brother, I would have seen what was going on with you before it was too late."

I shook my head. "Nah, man, my shit wasn't on you. I fucked up my life all on my own. Sorry, but you can't take credit for that."

"Still—"

"Nope. Not on you. I'm the one who went to that party. The one who let myself get talked into a single line of blow. The one who liked it so much I continued doing it so long that before I knew it, coke wasn't enough anymore. While you were undercover, you apparently did things you feel are worthy of self-flagellation, so don't take on my guilt. Give me that at least."

Brody sighed. "You're right. We both have our own sins to answer for."

I bit back the dickish reply on the tip of my tongue, because I knew he didn't mean anything by his comment. It was only the truth. Sin upon sin was piled on my shoulders. Not the least of which was the death of our mother. My intent may not have been to kill her, but I had nonetheless. That brought thoughts of Landon. Of our conversation that night.

Had she found the forgiveness she'd so desperately been seeking? Something told me she hadn't.

Seeing her again after all this time had been a shock. Discovering she'd been my brother's handler for nearly five years while he'd been undercover inside the cartel had been something else entirely. I didn't even want to think about what Brody would do if he learned she and I had history.

The fact our paths had crossed again meant something. She'd gotten away from me last week during the house-warming party, but I knew her real name. *Why had she given me a fake one anyway?* It was only one of many things about Landon Roberts I planned on finding out.

There was a sudden, soft knock on the door. My brother and I passed a surprised look between us. "Are you expecting anyone?"

He rose from his seat, shaking his head. "Not yet. We have an appointment scheduled for three this afternoon, but that's it."

A young woman stepped through the open door, and I couldn't hold back my shock. Neither could Brody.

"Michele, what are you doing here?" he asked.

"I need your help."

Brody and I exchanged another glance.

"I can pay you," she added at our hesitation.

"Don't worry about that right now. Why don't you have a seat?"

She perched on the edge of the chair Brody indicated.

"This is my brother, Preston."

Her gaze bounced between the two of us. "Michele and I met once before. Victor introduced us one night at *Sweet SINoritas* while he was looking for Álvarez. Although he may have left out the fact you and I are related."

"I see." He turned his attention back to her. "How did you find our office?"

"Ines. She's the only person I trust with this. She told me to come here and see you."

Since this involved his girlfriend, I let Brody keep control of the conversation.

"What sort of help do you need?"

She dug through the purse she'd laid in her lap. "Three weeks ago, one of the dancers from the club, Starla, OD'ed in the dressing room. I found this after Damon told me to clean out her locker."

Michele handed me the item. It was a small, plastic baggie with white residue inside. I didn't need to taste it to know it was cocaine. The sweet, almost floral scent was a dead giveaway. There was also a chemical smell I couldn't identify. For a brief second, my lids closed as the familiar aroma wafted around me. In a flash, I passed it off to Brody. I needed to get that shit away from me.

"Why are you bringing this here? You should take it to the police," I growled.

"I did. They looked at it and tossed it right back at me. Said they already knew what she'd died from. The asshole behind the desk barely even glanced at me."

Brody cleared his throat. "If the autopsy showed large amounts of cocaine in her system and they ruled an overdose as cause of death, then they didn't need this to prove it."

Michele's eyes teared up, but her clenched jaw and fists were pure rage. "There's been chatter around the club about a new drug on the streets. Something called *Rapture*. I overheard a few of the girls talking. Several of their friends and other people they know, including Starla, have all OD'ed using it."

I glanced over at the clear plastic in Brody's hand to see purple ink in the shape of wings decorating it.

She continued. "Starla was my friend. She didn't deserve to die. I want to find out who sold her this shit. They can't keep killing people without any consequence. It's obvious the cops couldn't care less. Especially not about some stripper. Which is why I came to you." She begged us with her eyes. "I need you to find out who's selling this and stop them."

CHAPTER 5

"YOU WANTED TO SEE ME, SIR?" I poked my head around Deputy Director Gibson's office door.

I hadn't been called in here since Brody resigned from the agency, and I'd been reassigned.

He waved me in. "Have a seat, Roberts."

I lowered myself to the chair and waited to hear what this was about. My nerves were stretched taut. Usually a meeting with Gibson was not for any good reason. *Shit. Was I about to get written up?*

"Have you seen this?" I reached for the object he held out to me. It was a small plastic baggie with purple angel wings stamped on it.

"No, sir." I was an Intelligence Research Specialist these days. A number cruncher and analyzer. I hadn't been out in the field in nearly a year. New narcotics were constantly being sold on the streets, but unless they moved beyond a specific quantity, with a high enough price tag, we left basic street drug sales to the local LEOs.

"It's supposedly called *Rapture*. A new, synthesized version of cocaine, but whatever chemicals they've added to it to increase the street value is lethal. I'm waiting on a component analysis from our forensic division. Reports from some of our agents on the streets are saying there's a significant rise in the movement of this shit."

What does that have to do with me? I didn't think my boss would appreciate the question so I asked a different one. "What is it you'd like me to do, sir?"

"Whatever you're working on, stop. From here on out, your priority is *Rapture*. I want you to find out where it's coming from. Who's supplying it. With Álvarez dead, and no one to lead the Juárez Cartel, Salazar and the Sinaloa Cartel have been moving into the city limits. Is it theirs? Our agents in the field haven't been able to locate a central supply source for this, but it's moving in massive quantities. Enough to catch our attention, but whoever is behind this is like a ghost."

My inner statistics nerd was geeking out over all the data he wanted me to go through, but the part of me that craved the rush of field work was itching for a chance to get back out there and track down some bad guys. I missed being a field agent. There was that rush of adrenaline making sure you weren't caught. The cloak and dagger methodology of finding hiding places out in the open and the passing of intel that led to arrests and getting drugs off the street and dealers behind bars. It wasn't necessarily where I saw myself all those years ago, but I was good at my job. I'd enjoyed it.

"Yes, sir. I'll do my best to get every bit of information I can. See if I can locate the source."

"Good. There are a couple narcotics officers at the local level who are working the case as well. I want you to coordinate an effort with them. See if we can't draw this son of a bitch out, and get this shit off the street."

Hearing the dismissal, I rose. "I'll speak to them and get back with you as soon as I have more information."

"See that you do. And, Roberts?"

I paused halfway out the door and looked at him over my shoulder.

"This is an election year. Part of the President's initiative is his anti-drug coalition. He wants to look really good to his constituents in the hopes of getting re-elected. Don't fuck this up."

So it was like that. I nodded. "Yes, sir."

After returning to my office, I booted up my computer. A small part of my job was to organize and study patterns of narcotics movement. Locate the frequency of deals, where they took place, and what narcotics were confiscated. I keyed in a few strokes and a blue and white digitized map of Chicago burst open onto the screen like a slide animation. Within the map were thousands and thousands of digital pins, color coded by the amount of substance obtained as well as which particular substance.

Selecting several filters, I was able to sort the data and zero in on more specific and detailed intel. I studied all the information and printed everything out. The office printer was down the hall, so I headed out there to grab the stack of papers, anxious to start combing through it all.

Just as I'd nearly made it back to my office, two people stepped around the corner, one of them colliding with me.

"Shit, Roberts. You all right?"

I glanced up to see Agents Royce Crawford and Eugene Brickman. "Hey, guys. Yeah, I'm fine. How's it going?"

The last time I'd seen the two of them was a month ago.

I'd called them right before the shootout at the warehouse where cartel leader Miguel Álvarez had been killed. They'd shown up to wait for the medical examiner and to confiscate all the cocaine stored in the surrounding warehouses.

"Not bad. We miss you out there with us." This came from Crawford.

A pang of envy hit me. The three of us had been in the same field unit, and we'd always worked well together. They'd had my back more than once. "Thanks, guys. I miss you too. Oh, hey, what do you know about this new drug, *Rapture*? Gibson wants me to find its source."

Brickman answered. "There's been chatter about it, but not enough we can get a solid lead on anything. I know the local narcs have a lot of intel on it, and they're keeping us in the loop, but our focus has been on Salazar and the Sinaloa Cartel moving into Chicago."

"Do you think it's theirs?" Even though copious amounts of cocaine had been linked to them, their biggest product was heroin. Also, giving a ridiculous street name to their coke didn't strike me as a cartel move. They didn't need some marketing gimmick to move their product.

"Nah, I don't think so. While I think there's a fuck ton of this stuff moving, enough to keep our eye on, I also don't think it's at Salazar's level," Crawford replied.

"Which means I'm starting from scratch. Thanks, guys. I'm going to start going through this stuff here," I motioned with the stack of papers against my chest. "Then I'm going to reach out to my contacts at the Chicago PD and see what intel I can get. Good to see you two again. Keep me in the loop if you hear anything, will ya?"

"You got it, Roberts. Don't get too lazy in that office of yours."

"Bite me, Brickman," I called over my shoulder with a smile. The echo of his laughter disappeared as they moved out of sight.

Once I was back at my desk, I picked up the phone and started making calls. Two hours later I had more information, but still, it wouldn't be enough to satisfy Gibson. I headed back to the Deputy Director's office. The door was still open. I knocked once.

"Back already, Roberts?"

No invitation to enter followed, so I remained in the doorway. "Yes, sir. I ran several reports and came up with a few patterns I feel need further investigating. I've also got a lead on several possible sources. I've spoken to my contacts at the Chicago PD, and they've been unable to provide any intel beyond what I've already discovered." This was where I hoped I wasn't going to regret things. "I know I requested the transfer to intelligence last year, and I'm happy serving in that capacity, but I think I can get more information returning to my previous position. Requesting permission to return to the field, sir."

It was a risk, asking for yet another transfer, but after my discussion with Crawford and Brickman, my mind refused to settle. I missed being out on the streets.

Based on Gibson's expression, he was none too happy about my request. Then again, he always had the look of someone who needed to take a shit but couldn't. I wasn't going to beg or plead. I was damn good at my job, and Gibson knew it.

"I'll submit the paperwork for the transfer in the morning."

Internally, I fist pumped the air, but on the outside, I

merely flashed a quick, small smile and nodded. "Thank you, sir. You won't regret it."

He waved me away, and I hustled back to my office, my body buzzing with an excitement I hadn't felt in a long time.

CHAPTER 6

I KEPT PICTURING that fucking baggie.

Michele had come and gone, and we had a surprising number of cases. Who knew there was such a high demand for private investigators in Chicago? Finally, though, the calls had stopped.

"You okay?"

"Hmm?" I blinked and glanced over at Brody. "Yeah."

"I'm going to talk to Ines. See if she can find out if there's a narcotics unit working on this. We'll pass it on to them."

Our first case, not that we'd officially taken it, but still, the first potential one, and it was about fucking drugs. It didn't surprise me that he didn't want to take this case. Money or no money. I couldn't let him do that though. Not because of me. I could handle this.

"No. Michele came to you because she trusts you to find out who is selling that shit and stop them."

He shook his head. "I saw how you reacted when she handed you that baggie. The flash of want in your eyes. No fucking way. It's not a good idea for so many reasons."

"When are you going to trust me?" That's what it boiled down to in the end. Was Brody going to turn down every case to come our way if there was any association with drugs?

Hurt dashed across his face.

"You think I don't trust you? I wouldn't have asked you to be my partner if I didn't. Believe me, I know how good it feels to take a hit. You're not the only one who has cravings. But I know how hard you've worked to stay clean. I don't want anything to derail that."

"And it won't. You know as well as I do that we're the best people to take this case. You have contacts in the D.E.A., and I have contacts out on the streets. Besides, the cops are overworked. Even the narc units probably don't have the time or resources to devote to this."

Brody's head dropped back so he could stare at the ceiling. The huff of expelled air told me I'd won.

I didn't dispute the fact that holding the clear plastic baggie in my fingertips hadn't brought out a tingle of need. The endorphin rush from blow was fantastic. Although nothing felt as good as a hit of black pearl running through my veins. The initial sting of the needle and then *whoosh*—complete and utter euphoria. But like I'd told Ines' brother Victor a couple months ago, there were things I wanted more than dope.

"Fuck." Our eyes met. "We'll take the case, on one condition."

"Name it."

"If, at any time, I feel like things are getting out of control, we're done. I won't let anything fuck up what we have here. Understand?"

"Understood."

"Alright. I still want to know what kind of info the local PD might have. Call Ines. See what she can find out from narcotics. I'm going to talk to Landon."

"You got it."

While Brody pulled out his phone to make his call, I dug out Ines' number and picked up the landline on my desk. If it wouldn't bring up a fuck ton of questions, I would have told Brody I'd call Landon instead of Ines.

I'd never been one to believe in fate, but the fact that she could be involved with this case had to be another sign. The universe was putting her in my path for a reason. I wasn't going to question what it could be. I planned on taking every advantage of it.

"Hello?"

"Hey, it's Preston."

"Oooh, how's business going?" Ines' excitement was cute. She was like a mom talking to her kid on his first day of school.

"Michele was here." Might as well get this over with.

Her attitude changed in a beat. "Oh my god, is she okay?"

I leaned forward in my chair, picked up the single pen, and habitually flicked the end on the desk. "She's fine. But Brody wanted me to call you. We need you to check with narcotics about a drug being sold called *Rapture*. Do they have any information on where it's coming from? Any questions they can answer about it would be helpful."

"Let me talk to Pablo. He works in narcs. I've only been back for a few weeks. After being gone almost a year, I'm pretty much starting from scratch. They have me back on patrol." I could hear the irritation in her tone.

"I appreciate it. As soon as you hear something, give me a call, will you?"

"Of course. Give me a few days, alright?"

"No problem. Thanks, Ines. Talk soon."

I'd never been a patient person. Brody was still on the phone, presumably with Landon. I planned on having my own discussion with her, even if I had to show up at D.E.A. headquarters to do it.

Finally he hung up.

"So, what did Landon have to say?"

"I got her voice mail. Left a message to call me back. What about Ines?"

Hmm, maybe I'd take a trip downtown after I left here for the day. I was pretty sure there was a little coffee shop on the corner of Dearborn and Jackson that offered the perfect view of her office building. Although, the more I thought this through, the more stalker-ish it seemed. Okay, probably not a good idea.

"Preston?"

Right, focus.

"She's going to talk to Pablo and get back to me. In the meantime, I have a suggestion you're not going to like."

Brody crossed his arms and waited, a leery expression on his face.

"I'm going to go talk to Terrance Larkins." I braced myself for the explosion in *three, two, one.*

"Are you out of your fucking mind?" My brother roared, jumping to his feet, fists slamming down on his desk, jarring the computer monitor and keyboard. I winced at the sound.

"The two of us go way back. Plus, you and I both know he has his ear to the ground. If anyone has information on who might be selling this stuff, it's Terrance."

"Because he's your goddamn drug dealer, Preston."

"*Was* my drug dealer. I haven't seen him in over a year."

"And you should be keeping it that way." Brody paced our small office while I sat quietly. It was best to let him get it out of his system. I was going to talk to Terrance. It would just be a whole lot easier having my brother on board. I understood the risks involved. All of them.

"This is something I need to do," I said quietly.

He stared at me. "Why? You're in a good place right now. *We're* in a good place. Why do you even need to put yourself in that kind of position?"

"Do you remember when mom died?"

Brody's shoulders sagged and he sank back in his chair. "Of course I remember."

I swallowed. Fuck this was hard. Twelve years and we'd never really talked about it.

"Well, I don't."

That brought him up short. "What do you mean?"

"I have flashes, but overall, I have no memory of what happened that day. I don't even know if the things I see are real or something my imagination created. Then, there's the black spots. The moments of time that are just…gone. I was blasted out of my fucking mind. Screams sometime sound in my head, but I don't know who they belong to. Or if it's merely my subconscious playing a sick joke on me." My gaze was unfocused, and I couldn't even make eye contact with him. Shame filled me, and acid churned in my gut.

"Jesus, Preston. I had no idea."

I rubbed the place on the right side of my chest where the small tattoo inked into my skin lay. The one that read *Louise Thomas* along with the date she was born and the date I'd killed her.

"I know." I sighed. "After that day, I got clean for the first time. Things changed. I got my shit together and you headed to Virginia and Quantico. God, you were determined. Almost obsessed with getting into the D.E.A. Because of me and what I'd done. You almost fucking died, Brody. Mom was already dead, and I nearly had your death on my conscience too."

"My cover being blown was not your fault. It just happened. And I didn't die. I'm here. With Ines. With you."

"I still would have felt responsible if I'd lost you. Which is why I need to do this. If I can help get rid of this one drug, then maybe it will make up for some of the things I've done. Which means talking to Terrance and seeing if he can give me something."

Brody threw his head back, his eyes staring at the ceiling. We both knew I was going. He just needed to come to terms with it. City sounds were faint through the windows but provided an almost soothing background noise to the tense and thick quiet inside our office. He'd finally come to peace with my decision, because his gaze met mine.

"I want it on record that I'm entirely against this." My mouth opened, but he held up his hand, and I clapped it shut again. "But I understand why you feel you need to do this. I just want you to be careful. I finally have my brother back, and I don't want to lose you again."

There was a tightness in my chest. "You won't, I promise."

Brody just nodded, but there was an uneasy tension between us the rest of the day.

CHAPTER 7

I'D GOTTEN Brody's message just as I was leaving for the day yesterday. There had been an edge to his tone, but he hadn't said it was an emergency. I'd spent all of last night once again going over the information I'd printed out.

As soon as I sat at my desk, I sent in a request to monitor a couple dealers that kept popping up. I wanted their phone records as well as video and audio surveillance. It would take a few days, at least, to get the approval. It would take at least that long for my request to be transferred to be complete anyway. The only thing I could do was sit back and wait. Something I'd never been any good at.

Which meant I should probably be returning that phone call.

"Brody Thomas."

"Hey, it's Landon. I got your message. Everything okay?"

"I'm not sure. Preston and I had a visitor yesterday."

My heart skipped a beat at the mention of his brother, but I forced a neutral tone to my question. "A visitor? Where?"

"At our office. Her name is Michele. She's one of the

strippers from the club where Ines danced while she was undercover."

"Your office? I didn't realize you'd opened already." He'd told me he and Preston were considering starting their own P.I. firm, but I hadn't given it much thought.

Brody chuckled. "Yesterday was our grand opening, and we've already got our first case. The first of a surprising amount actually."

"Well, good for you. I'm not sure why you're calling me, unless it's for a congratulations." I winced. "Sorry, I didn't mean it like that. You know I'm happy for you."

"I know. Don't worry about it." I could visualize him waving me off. "I'm calling because she brought with her an empty bag of coke she found after her girlfriend overdosed. Has an interesting marking on it."

All the hairs on the back of my neck stood on end as my eyes landed on the clear plastic still sitting on my desk. "What kind of marking?"

"From that tone, I think you know."

Fuck. "Why didn't she take it to the police?"

I was already keying the information into the database and pulling up data.

"Said she did, but they ignored her. The girl's cause of death had already been determined as an overdose. That's why she came to us. Ines sent her."

Brody was a civilian which meant I shouldn't even be talking to him at all, let alone possibly sharing confidential information from a federal agency. It didn't stop me from closing my office door and lowering my voice.

"Nothing I tell you goes any further than you and me. You got it?"

"Of course."

"I can't say a lot. Mostly because I don't know much. It's called *Rapture*. Gibson called me into his office yesterday. He wants me to find out everything I can about the substance. Who's selling it. Who's supplying it. We're blind, but based on the stats I've been running, this is huge. We're talking upper millions."

Brody pulled the phone away from his mouth, but I still heard him curse. Then he was back. "Preston talked to Ines yesterday. She's reaching out to the local narcs and seeing what she can find out about this shit. From what Michele said, word on the street is that a ton of girls are dying. I need to see if they've run any type of chemical composition on this stuff. See what they're cutting it with."

"Our lab tech guys have already done that. We're just waiting on the analysis report. I'll see what I can find out. I was left with a veiled threat."

"What kind of threat?" Brody growled.

"It's an election year."

"Gibson is a dick."

I had to laugh. Neither of them had been a fan of the other, so most of their communication had gone through me. "That may be true, but he's still my boss. I'm also going back out in the field in a few days. I've got some leads I plan on following up on. I know you'll do whatever it is you do on your end. Same as me. I'll share what I can, and I'm sure you'll do the same, but since you're a civilian, it won't be much."

"I understand. It's been a year since you've been an agent. Regardless of the time, things are different now. I just want you to be careful."

"I've got Crawford and Brickman watching my back."

"Good. They're both a bit uptight, but they know what

the fuck they're doing, and I trust them to help keep you safe. Keep me updated, okay?"

"I will."

"All right, I'll be in touch. Thanks, Landon."

For several minutes after hanging up, I sat there. Knowing Brody was involved changed things. Mostly, because that meant we might be able to work together again, which I'd missed. But he was a package deal. I wouldn't be working with just him. Seeing Preston had brought back emotions I'd spent too much time burying.

My initial reaction to hearing he and his brother had worked through their differences had been happiness. Brody loved his brother, and I'd seen over the years how much it hurt him that they weren't closer. But the fact they were partners in their own P.I. firm spoke volumes. Preston was helping people who needed it.

Aside from that brief meeting outside Brody's house last month, it had been two years since I'd talked to him. Had he become who he'd wanted? Had he forgiven himself?

I shook off the memories. No good would come of any of them. Instead, I pushed away all thoughts of Preston and that night and went back to work.

AFTER ONE FINAL STRETCH, I RUBBED MY EYES, TRYING TO EASE the strain behind them. I'd been staring at my computer screen for hours and getting nowhere. Or at least, not any further than where I'd gotten two hours ago. That was about the time I hit a dead end. It was pointless to keep sitting here doing nothing.

I'd been given the go-ahead to join Crawford and Brickman's team tomorrow. Gibson must have expedited the request. Which meant I needed to go home to get a good night's rest.

My nights were almost always plagued with nightmares. *Except that night with Preston.* The stupid voice mocked me. That had been one of the rare nights I'd fallen into a dreamless sleep. I'd woken up and for several moments I'd just stared at him. His face had been relaxed, and he'd looked so peaceful. From what Brody had told me, Preston was ten years younger than his brother, which would put him at five years younger than me.

For a moment, I'd imagined staying until he woke up. No doubt he'd have given me a few more orgasms. Maybe we would have had a cup of coffee or breakfast. But then what? It would have been an awkward goodbye.

I'd been selfish asking him to take away my pain. That pain was my penance. One I had to continue paying for the rest of my life.

I shut down my computer, grabbed my coat, slung my bag over my shoulder, and headed out the door. A heavy snow was falling outside, and I stopped for a moment to admire it. We were forecast to get at least eight inches of it by morning. Most people hated snow but not me. I appreciated the stark beauty of it. The cold was what I hated. My ideal vacation was cuddling up beneath a wool blanket inside a log cabin on a snow-covered mountain, with a roaring fireplace and hot cocoa in hand.

I picked up my pace and hurried down the sidewalk so I didn't miss my train. Just as my foot hit the first step of the staircase leading under the street, I heard his voice.

"Fancy meeting you here."

I glanced up and there, right on the other side of the

concrete wall, was Preston, beanie pulled down over his ears, his nose and cheeks bright red from the cold. My heart skipped, and I sucked in a breath before ignoring him and continuing down the stairs.

"Landon, wait."

What was he doing here? The traitorous part of me was happy to see him, but I squashed that. Was he stalking me? I tried to put as much distance between us as possible. If I was lucky, the train would arrive any second, and I could jump on before Preston managed to catch up with me.

Seeing the empty platform told me my luck had run out. Shit. I stood there, my foot tapping an irritated beat.

"Running again, I see."

My lids dropped closed as that bourbon-smooth voice rolled through me. Pasting on the mask I got so tired of wearing, I swiveled my head in his direction.

"What do you want, Preston?" I was proud of how steady the question came out, because my insides were trembling. Despite the noxious odor of the subway station, I still caught a whiff of that goddamn spring and sunshine scent of his. It was meant to torment me.

"I want to know why you ran. Why the fake name?" He sighed heavily and those hazel eyes of his studied me.

Seeing.

Knowing.

Hurting.

I shifted my weight, uncomfortable under his intense scrutiny.

"I just want to know why."

I took in everything about him. Preston hadn't changed much since that night. He'd been slender back then, but he'd definitely filled out some. Not so hollowed cheeks. A bit bulkier in the shoulders. He also seemed a little more at peace.

My head turned until I was no longer looking at him, because I couldn't stand to see the confusion in his gaze. "It was better for both of us." Which was the truth.

"I don't think you're the only one who gets to decide what's best."

The screeching of bad brakes pierced the air, echoing in the enclosed chamber surrounding us until the lumbering beast came to a halt. The pneumatic doors hissed before opening. People spilled out of the cars. In five steps I was inside and pivoted to see Preston still standing on the platform, his eyes locked on mine.

"In this case, I do. Let it go." Let *me* go. Those last words were unspoken, but he flinched as though I'd said them out loud. After another hiss, the doors closed, but I could still see him clearly through the Plexiglas, staring at me with an expression I couldn't read. With a jerk, the train darted way, putting much needed distance between us.

CHAPTER 8

FOR TWO DAYS, I couldn't stop thinking about my run-in with Landon inside the subway station. Not that it had been accidental. I'd needed to see her, talk to her, again. She'd been so determined outside Brody's house all those weeks ago that our night together hadn't been more than a casual fuck.

I'd seen the pain she'd tried to hide. It had been in her rigid posture, in the way she'd refused to look me in the eye. Her casual dismissiveness was a protective move. I just didn't know why. Unless it was her alleged sins. The one she'd told me she needed forgiveness for.

More than anything, I wanted her to trust me with them, but there was no way that would happen if she kept pushing my away. *Why did I care so much?*

I kept asking myself.

I still didn't haven't an answer.

But the one thing I was sure of was that no matter how much she denied it, the connection between us that night had been real.

I needed to stop thinking of her and start focusing on the

meeting I was heading to. Despite my reassurances to Brody that it would all be fine, I'd admit to being nervous for a lot of reasons. Not the least of which was the fact that I was about to have a face-to-face with my former dealer. *What the fuck had I been thinking?* Despite my promise to Brody that coming here wouldn't be a problem, I couldn't stop that tiny, insidious voice from whispering in my ear.

No one will ever know. Just a little bit. For old time's sake.

I parked my toasty warm car along the curb of the one-way street under the shade of a giant maple tree just like the old days. The quiet neighborhood in the Lake View area of Chicago was straight out of *Better Homes and Gardens*. During the summer, the lawns were a bright, Kelly green and perfectly manicured. Although calling them lawns was generous.

Street after street was lined with shotgun houses. Like dominoes, they were placed so close together, one neighbor could reach out of their kitchen window and nearly touch the house next to them. But the majority of them had a small grassy area in front. A few, like the one I was walking to, were set off to themselves, surrounded by a wrought iron fence.

The glaring sun was a disguise for the bitter cold air surrounding me. I tugged my beanie down a little further over my ears and shuddered as a chill snaked its way past my collar to slither along my spine. It didn't help I was only a block from the lake, which only exacerbated the fucking freezing temps Chicago was feeling right now.

The two-story house stood out from the rest of the neighborhood. From its bright white siding that dirt wouldn't dare cling to, to its painted black shutters, it was obvious the owners spent a lot of money on its upkeep.

Despite the fact we were most definitely in winter the manicured lawn still maintained, if not the bright green of summer, a lighter green, as opposed to the brown shade of death.

With a faint clang, I let the gate close behind me, and I took the steps up to the front door. The people on the other side knew I was there before I knocked. I didn't glance in any direction but forward. The back of my neck burned knowing that numerous unseen cameras were following every step I'd taken, the second I'd reached the property. Despite the fact my presence was detected, I rapped on the wood in front of me. My hand trembled, and I shoved it in my coat pocket. I counted to ten before I heard the sound of the first of many deadbolts disengaging. The door opened to a familiar, diminutive man wearing a suit. No one would ever guess he was a former assassin.

"Can I help you?" His greeting was polite, but cool.

"I'm here to see Mr. Larkins." I was proud of the fact my voice came out confident and strong.

"May I tell him who's calling?"

"Preston Thomas." As if Carlisle didn't already know who I was. But this was how it was done.

The small man bowed. "Please wait here. I'll see if he's available."

I inclined my head, and he disappeared down a hallway that branched off the high-ceilinged foyer. I didn't remove my coat, but I slid my beanie off my head and tucked it in my pocket. My eyes traveled around the room.

Everything about the entryway was the same as the last time I'd been here. A three-tiered crystal chandelier hung from the center, each light brightly lit and sparkling like a flawless diamond. Each of the four six-paneled windows along the rear wall was washed clean without a single streak marring its surface.

The white marble floor was polished to a shine that rivaled the sun. Paintings by long-dead famous artists decorated the walls, their bright colors standing out against the paleness of the rest of the room. Standing here, once again, in the same spot I'd stood so many times before sent conflicting emotions bouncing through me.

Footsteps grew louder until they echoed through the cavernous entryway, and Carlisle reappeared.

"Mr. Larkins will see you." He turned away again, not offering to take my coat. Which was fine. I didn't plan on being here that long. I followed him down a long hallway, bisected by a short hallway. A right turn led us to our intended destination.

The door was open and given a gesture to enter, I stepped into the giant office. It smelled of cigar and a faint hint of pine. A solid bookcase stood against the wall to my left with rows and rows of books lining the shelves. There was a towering grandfather clock against another wall, its brass pendulum swinging back and forth, the faint *tick-tock* a background noise to the room.

But the presence of the man behind the desk was what drew my full attention. He was in his late forties, with salt-and-pepper hair and matching mustache and goatee. His navy, pinstriped three-piece suit no doubt cost more than I'd make in a year. Power radiated from him despite being seating. Even the hulking bodyguard positioned in the corner didn't catch as much attention.

"Mr. Thomas, it's been a long time." He didn't offer me a seat.

"Over a year."

"And how may I help you today?"

I'd debated how I was going to handle today's meeting. Aside from the cartel, Larkins was one of the leading heroin dealers in Chicago, catering to the addictions of the rich and famous. His dope was the highest grade product out there.

"I was hoping you could provide me some information." If I hadn't known Terrance Larkins for nearly eight years, I wouldn't dare ask for his assistance.

He leaned forward and rested his chin on steepled fingers. I didn't blink or glance away no matter how long he continued to stare at me. Several minutes passed before finally, with a bark of laughter, he leaned back and relaxed in his chair. "Always did have balls the size of cantaloupes, didn't ya Preston? Have a seat and tell me about this information you're looking for."

I sank into the plush leather chair on this side of his desk.

"I recently went into business with my brother. We started our own PI firm."

"Congratulations. I'm glad to see the two of you have worked out your differences. I know how much Brody means to you." Terrance intentionally used my brother's name. He knew who, and what, my brother was. It wasn't necessarily a threat. More like a subtle reminder. "I'm still not sure what that has to do with me."

"Apparently there's this new shit product out there called *Rapture*. No one knows where it's coming from. I was hoping you might be able to lead me in a direction." I remained still and relaxed while he studied me.

His posture didn't change, but there was definitely a shift in the air surrounding him. "I assume this has something to do with your new business venture?"

I nodded. "A stripper came to us after one of her girl-friends overdosed. Asked for our help."

It had been a calculated risk coming here. Like Terrance said, it was pretty ballsy of me. But, if he gave me what I was asking for, then it was worth it. I didn't say anything further. Just waited on whatever decision he would come to. Either he gave me something or he didn't.

The *tick-tock* sound from the grandfather clock seemed excessively loud while neither of us spoke. I started counting along. *One-tick, two-tock, three-tick, four-tock, five-tick.*

I'd reached eighteen-tock before he broke the silence. "I've always liked you Preston. You aren't messy, and you know how to keep your mouth shut. I admire those traits in people."

He paused, yet I continued remaining quiet. I'd learned over the years the appropriate time to speak to a man like Terrance Larkins, and this was definitely not one of those times. It was my acknowledgment to his power and control over our conversation. Finally, he spoke again.

"I scratched and clawed my way out of the gutters of this fucking city. Built this empire from almost nothing. That doesn't mean that I've forgotten where I came from. Forgotten about my friends who still live on those streets." He leaned forward again, resting his forearms along the desktop in front of him. "I offer my customers a high-quality product, because I remember watching people, friends, die on some dirty mattress in a rat-infested building from bad shit."

Terrance's gaze was glassy and unfocused. Was he thinking of those dead friends now? He blinked and his eyes landed back on me. "I recommend you visit *Club Delight*."

Nothing else was forthcoming so I took that as my cue that this conversation was over.

"Thank you." I rose from the chair. I'd gotten what I'd come for. It wasn't much, but it was more than I expected. It was up to Brody and me to figure things out from here. "I appreciate you taking the time to see me, Mr. Larkins."

I pivoted to show myself out. I knew the way.

"Oh, and Preston?"

I paused just outside the door of his office and glanced back to see the ruthless drug lord staring back at me. "My generosity only extends so far. The next time you come here asking for information, I'll have Jake here go say hello to that lovely cop girlfriend of your brother's. Are we clear?"

I didn't flinch, merely inclined my head in acknowledgment, before walking out the front door, my palms sweating as I swallowed back the nausea. Brody was right. It had been a mistake to come here.

CHAPTER 9

PRESTON HAD COME to me in a dream last night. Only it was unlike one I'd ever had before. I'd been standing next to a lily-pad covered lake, sunlight peeking through the newly budding trees that surrounded me. It was quiet, except for the birds singing and the occasional croaking frog. I was on the stair-staggered rock formation looking out over the water, and I felt a presence behind me. I hadn't been scared, though.

Strong arms circled my waist, and I angled my head as lips brushed a soft kiss against the side of my neck. I inhaled deeply, the familiar scent of new beginnings and rebirth filling my nose. I didn't turn in his arms. Just leaned back into the solid chest as his arms tightened. Peace flowed through me. At least I thought it was peace. I'd never felt it before. We'd stood there in silence until I'd woken up, my pillow damp from the tears I'd spilled in my sleep.

After that, I couldn't go back to sleep. Instead, I'd laid there for the rest of the night trying to figure out what the dream had meant. I hadn't seen the man's face, but I'd smelled the long-remembered cologne and seen the tattoos on the arms he'd held me safely in. Even without the ink, I would have known it was him. No one before in my life had ever made me feel protected like Preston had.

Hours later, I still had no idea what the dream meant. My alarm went off at six, and I dragged myself out of bed. That had been four hours ago. I'd made it to work, checked in with Brickman and Crawford, and I was on my way over to Wacker Street to follow a lead.

Club Delight had popped up during a search where several drug busts had taken place over the last six months. During the most recent ones, the narcotic confiscated had been *Rapture*. The only information the local cops had been able to get from the seller was a first name: Felipe. Which wasn't much to go on, but it was a start. Which was why I was here.

The door closed behind me, blocking out most of the sunlight. I stood in a dim room with only a scant amount of light coming through the painted over windows and artificial, fluorescent lighting from the ceiling. As I moved through the open area, the stench nearly overwhelmed me. It smelled like yeast and vomit. I stepped over an unidentified substance on the floor with my fingers under my nose trying not to gag.

People actually enjoyed coming to this lovely den of disgust? Elliott King clearly had a twisted sense of humor naming this place *Club Delight*, because it was anything but delightful. It was nasty. I wasn't normally a germaphobe, but Jesus, I was afraid to touch anything.

Closed until tonight, the club was empty of the sweaty mass of gyrating bodies that were normally packed in here. The shelves behind the bar were fully stocked with bottle after bottle of nearly every liquor imaginable; well along the bottom row to top shelf that, even on tip toe, I probably couldn't reach.

"Can I help you?" A bald man carrying a crate full of bottles had stepped through an open doorway to the left of the bar. Given his narrow-eyed glare, he didn't appear too happy to see me, especially after his gaze landed on the badge clipped to the waist of my jeans. "Agent…?"

"Roberts," I finished his question.

After setting down his load, he crossed his arms and leaned against the bar. "Again, what can I do for you Agent Roberts?"

"I'm looking for Elliott King."

"Not here."

"Do you know when he *will* be here or where I might be able to find him?"

He shrugged. "Couldn't tell ya. I'm not his secretary."

Wiseass. I pasted on my most pleasant smile. "I see. Well maybe you can help me then, Mr…?"

"Doubtful." His stern expression didn't shift. He merely continued staring me down, ignoring my question. I took my time studying him. He wasn't threatening, just not forthcoming.

"Well, since you aren't a secretary, are you the manager, then?"

"Nope, just the bartender."

"I've been to enough bars to know there's no such thing as 'just the bartender'." My smile became a little more genuine. "You're a confidante. Someone they can trust. You're also the one who knows more than everyone else in this place."

"Well, when you put it that way." He smirked, one side

LK SHAW

of his mouth pulling up in a half smile. "Sorry I was being a dick. Grant Marsden."

He shifted away from the wall and began putting away the bottles of beer he'd brought out from the back room.

"Mr. Mars—"

"Just Grant." He shook his head, cutting me off. "Mr. Marsden is my father."

"Grant, then. Like I said, you're probably the person I should be directing my questions to anyway. If anyone has the answers, I'm sure it's you."

He was still wary. "Like I said, doubtful."

"Let's try anyway. Have you ever heard of something called *Rapture*?"

There was a flicker of recognition in his eyes before it disappeared. "Afraid not."

"What about the name Felipe? Does that sound familiar?"

Another flicker. "There are a lot of people who come in and out of this place. I don't know the names of even half of them."

"And what about the other half?"

He stacked rocks glasses upside down on top of each other. "Agent Roberts, I come to work, serve drinks, get my pay, and walk out the door. I keep my questions and my curiosity to myself."

"I see."

Grant opened and closed his mouth like he wanted to say something. I didn't push. Just let him decide what he was going to do. He must have made a decision, because he opened his mouth again. "Unlike one of the other bartenders."

"What do you mean?"

"He started acting weird the last few days he was here. Lots of secretive phone calls. Jumpy and on edge. I'd caught him a few times trying to listen in on conversations between Mr. King and a couple of guys in the back room. Then, about two weeks ago, he didn't show up for work one night. Haven't seen him since."

"Do you know what happened to him? Or who the two other guys were?"

Grant shook his head. "No. And I'm pretty sure I don't want to."

"Does this bartender have a name?" I pulled out a notebook. "No one will know you're the one who told me. But I'm trying to save people's lives, Grant. It's possible Mr. King has information regarding the sale of this *Rapture*."

He shrugged. "No offense, Agent Roberts, but I'm sorry I can't help you. If you want answers to your questions, I recommend you get a warrant."

Beneath his bravado, there was also fear. If what he said about the other bartender was true, then it was possible he had reason to be afraid.

The front door opened behind me, and I spun on my heel, my hand instinctively going for my gun. Sun blinded me briefly.

"Preston?" My voice rose in shock. "What are you doing here?"

I shoved back the part of me that reared to life at seeing him.

"I'm here following a lead. I assume you're here for the same reason."

"Yes, but no luck."

His chin jerked in Grant's direction. "He not talking?"

I turned back to the bartender. "I'll be back with a

warrant." It wouldn't be easy securing one without probable cause, but I'd do my best. "Thank you for the information. Here's my card. If the name of that other bartender comes to you, give me a call, will you?"

He took my card with a nod. I made my way to the door, taking care with my footsteps, unable to avoid walking past Preston.

"Agent Roberts."

We both turned back at my name.

"I believe Mr. King spends a lot of time at Monteverde over on Madison."

I nodded in appreciation and stepped out into the cold, ignoring the man hot on my heels.

"So, is that where we're going next?"

Turning on my heel, I glared at Preston, who stood grinning like he was having a great time. "We're not going anywhere."

"Why not?"

"Because. This is official federal agency business, and you're a civilian. That's why."

He scoffed. "I'm a private investigator who's…investigating. I came here looking for information on *Rapture*, which, I'm pretty sure, is why you came here. Now we get to take a field trip."

"For god's sake, Preston," I snapped. "This isn't some joke. People are fucking dying from this shit, and you're not even taking it seriously."

An instant shift came over him, and I unconsciously took a step back at the anger on his face.

"Don't you think I know people are dying? I could have been one of them. I nearly have been. More than once. So believe me, I'm very much taking this seriously, Landon."

The slight heat of shame stung me. I'd overreacted and had been shitty, but I couldn't think clearly when he was this close. "I'm sorry. I shouldn't have said that."

His expression relaxed, and he rubbed a hand down his face. "No, I'm sorry. I shouldn't have yelled at you like that."

An awkward silence hung between us. I shifted nervously on my feet. "What were you doing here anyway? I mean at *Club Delight*? You said to investigate, but what made you come here, specifically?"

"I asked around for where I might be able to find information on *Rapture*."

My arms crossed over my chest. "And just who happened to give you this information?"

Preston avoided my gaze. "It doesn't matter. The only thing that matters is that you didn't get the information either of us needed. So, we'll keep looking."

I sighed. He wasn't getting it. "There is no 'we'. I keep telling you this, but you're not listening."

He stepped right into my personal space, his chest nearly brushing mine. Instant heat spread through me. My breath caught as he reached up and cupped my cheek. "You can lie to yourself all you want, but there is most definitely a we, Landon. You're just fighting it."

Damn him. Why did he keep doing this to me? *Why did I keep letting him?* "Can we not have this conversation right now?" I sighed. "Please?"

Preston's lips tightened and his jaw clenched, but his hand dropped, and cold air hit my cheek that was quickly losing the warmth from his touch. "Fine, but we *will* have it."

I nodded, grudgingly accepting the fact. It was obvious

that he wasn't going to give up easily. I might as well resign myself to it.

"Let me do my job. I already told Brody I would share what I could with you guys."

"Which I'm sure you will. But I need to do my job too. I have a personal stake in this case."

I understood where Preston was coming from, but we, *I*, needed distance. "You and Brody can run your investigation however you'd like. Unless you get in my team's way, there's nothing I can do to stop you. But I can't just have you tagging along with me wherever I go. It doesn't work that way."

Finally, he nodded, and I let out the breath I'd been holding. "I just don't want you to get hurt."

"While I appreciate your concern, I've been doing this a long time."

"That may be, but I just found you. I don't want to lose you again."

My heart ached. I couldn't do this right now. "I need to get back to work."

I turned and walked away, praying he wouldn't stop me, yet there was a small part of me that wanted him to ask me not to go. He cursed, but didn't follow.

CHAPTER 10

I'D BEEN SHOCKED as hell to walk into the club this morning and see Landon in there. I'd missed her discussion with the bartender, but I'd enjoyed watching how confidently she stood there. She was so different from the woman I'd met at that hotel bar. I was trying to reconcile the two.

I hadn't lied when I said we were going to talk, but in the meantime, I was back inside *Club Delight*. Landon may need a warrant, but I didn't. The bartender knew something. I'd shown up a little early, around ten, and stood in line out in the cold for far too fucking long before finally being allowed inside.

I strolled around the edge of the dance floor, the flashing lights exposing and then hiding a myriad of sins going on. The music was making my ears bleed. Whatever kind of techno-shit they were playing in this place was awful. Was this really what people were listening to these days? Jesus.

It had been about six years since I'd been in a club like this. Not that I remembered much about my time spent in one. I'd been too busy in the bathroom sticking a needle in my arm.

There were three bartenders behind the bar, including the guy from this morning. I wasn't sure if he'd recognize me or not. I hoped he'd been paying more attention to Landon than he had been to me. I was about to find out.

Squeezing my way between bodies, I made my way up to the bar.

"I don't have anything to say to you." He had to lean forward and raise his voice to be heard over the trash coming from the DJ booth.

"I'm just here for a drink, man," I shouted back. "Can I get a Johnny Walker Black?"

He hesitated before finally grabbing a rocks glass. A few minutes later I dropped a twenty on the bar, sipped my scotch, and tried not to gag. *Nasty stuff.* I leaned back against the curved edge of wood and stared out at the gyrating bodies.

I could read body language. I noticed the furtive glances of twitchy cokeheads sniffing and wiping their noses. I watched everyone, looking for tells. *Bingo.*

My eyes landed on a scrawny kid in his early twenties, standing against the wall near the hallway that led to the bathrooms. He was antsy and bouncing back and forth on his toes. His gaze was frantic, like he was desperately searching for someone. I eased off the bar and made my way toward him.

"How's it going, man?"

He glared at me. "Fuck off. I'm waiting for someone, and you're going to scare him off."

"Maybe you're waiting for me."

"You're not Felipe. Now get the hell away from me."

I slowly sipped my drink, feeling the burn of an alcohol I hadn't touched in two years. "Oh, I've heard of him. Do you think maybe you could hook me up? I hear he's got this new shit that gives you a high like no other."

The coker eyed me up and down and jerked his chin in my direction. "You a cop?"

I discreetly showed him my arm. "Do I look like a cop to you?"

He took in my scars before meeting my eyes again. Then he glanced away, his gaze darting around the room. Without looking at me, he spoke out of the side of his mouth. "What you looking for?"

"I keep hearing about this shit *Rapture*. Can your friend get me some?"

"Are you kidding? He's the main man for that."

I took another sip of my scotch. "How much can I get for $25?"

Sniff. "Shit, I can get you a dime bag for that."

"The fuck? A dime bag is like ten bucks, man."

"Shhh," he waved his hand at me. "Keep your goddamn voice down. You said you wanted the good shit. Well, that's how much it costs."

I didn't know who was playing who, but if this Felipe was charging that much for a fucking dime bag, he was making bank. Especially for bad shit.

"Fine, whatever. Now, where is this friend of yours anyway?"

The kid looked around, wiping his nose, his gaze back to scanning the room. "Fuck, dude, you probably scared him off thinking you were a goddamn pig."

There was no way this Felipe guy thought I was a cop.

And even if he did, he'd send one of his men to approach and ask a few pointed questions.

But the kid was right. He may not be scared, but until he actually figured out who I was, he was being cautious. Which was fine. I wasn't going anywhere yet.

"Well, I'll leave you alone. But if you see your friend. Let him know I'm interested in a business transaction."

I didn't really expect him to even remember half of our conversation. But this club had eyes and ears, and if I were lucky, the message would find its way to Felipe. In the meantime, I was going to head back over to the bar and wait. It may not be tonight, but eventually I'd make contact.

TWO HOURS LATER I TOOK THE LAST SWALLOW OF THE SAME watered-down scotch I'd ordered upon my arrival. It would seem I'd be making an appearance at the lovely *Club Delight* another night since this one was a bust. I plunked down my empty glass on the bar top and headed toward the door. Before I got halfway there, someone ran into me, knocking my shoulder backward. I held up my hands even though I hadn't been at fault. "Hey, man, sorry about that."

"I hear you're looking for Felipe?"

"Maybe. Who's asking?"

"Don't worry about what my name is."

"Then don't worry about who I was or wasn't looking for." I started moving toward the door again, blowing off the guy who most definitely knew my soon-to-be new friend, Felipe.

"Do you want to meet him or not?"

Keeping my smile to myself, I slowly pivoted back around. "I don't follow people whose names I don't know."

He grunted. "Name's Cruz. And you are?"

"Preston."

"This way, then, Preston."

I followed the Latinx man, maneuvering between bodies until we reached the far side of the club. A horseshoe-shaped booth surrounded a circular table. Seated on the booth were several women, all wearing skin-tight dresses with their tits popping out the top and that barely covered their ass. Their heavy makeup was unattractive. Sitting in the gaggle of women was an equally unattractive man. Oily, slicked back hair and wearing a pin-striped suit. He was smoking a cigar and had a woman tucked under his arm. He gestured toward the single open chair across from him. I took a seat, leaned back, and crossed my ankle over my knee.

"I understand you were asking about me." His accent was pure Chicagoan.

"Depends on whether or not you're Felipe."

He chuckled low as though I'd said something funny. A plume of smoke exited his mouth. "And if I am?"

I shrugged as if I didn't care. "Then I guess you're who I'm looking for."

A slap came to the back of my head, hard enough to make it snap forward. I jumped out of my chair, nearly knocking it over, and with one smooth motion I spun with a left hook and clocked the bastard on the jaw. Feminine cries echoed around me despite the volume of the music from the speakers. "You fucking touch me again, and next time it'll be a knife you feel. You understand me?"

The sound of a fake golf clap came from behind me. "Bravo. Not many people would dare hit Cruz, here."

"Yeah, well, I don't give a shit who he is. No one lays a hand on me."

Felipe inclined his head, but otherwise didn't acknowledge my command. "Now that we've gotten the pleasantries out of the way, how about introductions? You know who I am, but why don't you tell me who you are?"

I glared at Cruz for a second longer before returning to my seat. "My name is Preston."

He was silent, studying me the same way I was studying him, his glance darting to my arms before returning to my face. "And what can I do for you?"

"I was hoping we could do a little business."

"What kind of business are you referring to?"

"Supply and demand."

Felipe gave me a small, half-smile. "I'm not sure I have the supply you're looking for."

"That's fine." I shrugged. "I still have a few people on the streets I used to know. I'm sure they'd be happy to be introduced to my other friend, Ben Franklin. Thank you for your time."

I started to rise, but he waved me back down. Slowly, I sank back into my seat.

"Maybe we can work something out. But not tonight."

"You tell me when and where."

"It's going to be a day or two. Give Cruz your number and wait for his call."

I should have expected this. It wasn't that I didn't have a phone, but I no longer had a phone specifically for this type of situation. I was going to have to give my number to him though if I wanted this to go any further. *Fuck.* I'd have to figure something out later. I held out my hand for Cruz's phone. He passed it off, and I keyed my number into it.

"Now that we have that settled, how about a drink?"

"I appreciate the offer, but I was actually on my way out." Not waiting for a response, I rose again from the chair and made my way back through the pool of bodies on the dance floor. Snagging my coat from the coat check, I headed out into the cold, trying to figure out how to tell Brody what I'd just done.

Was I getting myself in deeper than I could handle?

CHAPTER 11

I'D BEEN SEEING Dr. Rose Carpenter since just after I'd turned twenty. My pediatric shrink had referred me to her once she felt I'd aged out of her services. We'd had a rocky start, but over the last fourteen years she'd become invaluable to me.

While I didn't always care for her analysis of my feelings or how she pushed me to make my own analysis of them, I respected her and her opinion.

My meds were almost gone, and I needed a refill, which was one of the reasons I was here. Plus, I really needed to talk to her.

The low buzz from some talk show provided a white noise background in the waiting room. I flipped through an issue of *Cosmo* without really seeing anything on the pages. I had no interest in pictures of stick-thin models wearing outfits no regular human being would wear, even if they could afford the price tag.

Or ridiculous articles like *"Twenty ways to bring a man to his knees (and to your bed)"*. I shook my head. You didn't need twenty ways. Just flash your tits and you were golden. Why did people have to make shit complicated?

The office door opened and out stepped Dr. Carpenter. "Afternoon, Landon. Why don't you come on back?"

Setting down the magazine, I trailed her to her office. She gestured to the soft leather chair while she smoothed her skirt beneath her and took her own seat.

"How are things since the last time we spoke? You'd just had a run-in with a man from your past. Have you seen him again?"

I nearly laughed at her description of Preston. A man from my past didn't even begin to describe him.

"I've had a few, unfortunately."

"And how did you feel seeing him again?"

I shifted in my chair. There wasn't an answer I wanted to admit to.

"Landon?"

"I don't know," I said, just to give her something.

Dr. Carpenter merely leaned back in her chair. "You said there were a few run-ins. Were these accidental meetings?"

"Definitely showing up where I was interviewing someone was." I thought about it for a minute. "The subway? I don't think so. It seemed a little too coincidental."

"You still didn't answer my other question. How did you feel seeing him?" She smiled to soften the chastisement.

Dr. Carpenter had been working with me long enough to know that I often avoided the questions I wasn't ready to answer. This was most definitely one of them. "I truly don't know."

She studied me, and I tried not to squirm under her penetrating gaze. "How have you been sleeping?"

Not that this topic was any better, but I was glad we'd

moved on from Preston. Although it wasn't a permanent shift of topics. We'd revisit it again. "Same as always. I have good nights and bad nights."

"Is the medication you're taking to help you sleep not working?"

"I don't always like taking it. It makes me feel like a zombie. Makes me sluggish the next day."

Dr. Carpenter grabbed a pad of paper and pencil off the desk behind her and started making notes. "We can try to adjust the dosage. Or find something different. If it's altering your mental status, then we need to look at options."

"Maybe something different."

She nodded and placed the pad in her lap. "So you said you have good and bad nights. I know during the bad ones you've said that sometimes this man from your past features in your dreams. Is that still the case?"

"Yes," I conceded.

Dr. Carpenter nodded like she'd already known my answer. "Often emotions manifest themselves in our dreams in different ways. What about this man? What emotion does he represent?"

I heaved a frustrated sigh. "I told you, I don't know."

"I think you do know," she pressed.

"It doesn't matter what he represents." My fists clenched in my lap, and my chest burned like fire.

"Why not?"

"Because it doesn't. Now stop pushing me," I snapped.

Dr. Carpenter's lips tightened, and she remained silent for a moment. "We'll stop discussing this for today, because it's obvious you're not ready to confront how he makes you feel. I understand. But I also want you to consider why you're not ready. What is it about him that scares you?"

Because he makes the pain go away. Pain I deserve to feel. But I didn't tell her either of those things. I kept them locked away inside me.

"How's your journaling going?"

I relaxed into my chair at the change of topic. My muscles ached from the tension I'd been holding in them. This was a safe topic. Writing my feelings down wasn't my favorite thing to do, but it did help me get rid of some of the shit in my head.

"It's fine. I've been writing a lot more lately, it seems like."

"Are you going back and rereading your entries? Seeing if you can spot any consistencies or patterns in what you're writing and feeling and what the feelings connect to?"

Maybe this wasn't such a safe topic. "Yes."

The expression on Dr. Carpenter's face was one of patient expectation. "And? Are you finding any?"

All my scribblings in my journal before the last few weeks had to do with my dad. But ever since then, they've all been directly connected to Preston.

"Yes."

I saw her disappointment that I wasn't going to elaborate. It was pure stubbornness at this point, but my emotions were all tangled up right now, and I needed to sort them out before I was ready to talk about them. Dr. Carpenter studied me. Whatever she saw on my face had her giving up pushing me. I was grateful for it.

"How about we call it a day? But, Landon? As much as you don't want to acknowledge how you feel towards this man, it's important that you do. You need to admit why these feelings scare you. Compartmentalizing them is not good for you."

I gave a brief nod that I understood what she was saying. Standing, she moved to the back of her desk and pulled a pad out of her drawer, scribbling across it. "Here's a prescription for a different sleep aid, as well as a 'script for a refill of your other medications." She tore off the sheet and handed it to me. "I'd like to see you back here in two weeks. You can make an appointment with Gretchen before you leave."

"You do know I appreciate all you've done for me. I'm probably not your easiest patient." I gave her a self-deprecating smile.

"I know it's hard for you, but you've come so far. You should be proud."

"Thanks, Doc."

She nodded. "We'll see you soon."

After I'd stopped by the receptionist desk and scheduled my appointment, I headed home. Sherbert greeted me with his usual chirp. After grabbing a beer from the fridge, I pulled out my journal and curled up on my sofa, tugging the throw over my legs. The cat settled in behind my knees. Absently, I scratched his head while I read back over my last week's worth of entries.

Every single one was about Preston. About that night. About each time I'd seen him over the last couple months. The initial, knee-jerk emotion I'd felt each of those times. But I'd also jotted down why I had to stay away from him.

CHAPTER 12

"THOMAS BROTHERS, P.I., can I help you?"

"Listen to you sounding all official with your 'Thomas Brothers, P.I.'," Ines dropped the pitch of her voice on the name to try and mimic me and then giggled on the other end of the phone. I couldn't help smiling. She sure was getting a kick out of Brody and me being in business together.

It was nice having a sister. Her brothers, on the other hand, especially Victor, who'd actually become a good friend, were nearly as bad as my own brother in regards to being over-protective.

"I hope you're calling with news from Pablo."

"Yes, and no."

I didn't like the sound of that. "Spill it, Ines."

"He said the narcs unit has noticed increased drug activity at this place called *Club Delight*, which is owned by local millionaire, Elliott King. Mr. King owns multiple clubs, restaurants, and a few other various businesses, including a trucking and delivery company. Unfortunately, they haven't been able to tie any activity to him. Not even remotely. He's squeaky clean. Almost too clean, if you ask me." She sighed in frustration. "The only thing they've managed to get are a couple names, Felipe and Cruz. Pablo said he doesn't know every dealer on the street, but he can almost swear these guys are new. Like they just came onto the scene at the same time this *Rapture* shit did. Only problem is, they can't confirm they're the ones selling the stuff, and neither have been arrested during any of the deals at the club. Other than that, that's all he has."

"Damn it." I collapsed back into my chair. "I pretty much found all that out by myself already. I'm doing my own investigating from the club angle. From what I've discovered so far, Felipe seems to be just a low-end street dealer, and Cruz is his muscle. He's like the sales clerk who answers to a manager, who answers to the owner."

I still hadn't told Brody about my visit to the club the other night. I planned on waiting until I got the call from Cruz. Was it a pussy thing to do? Yes, but I'd rather save the fighting until the last minute. "But, low-level or not, I think he's smart."

"What do you mean you're working that angle?" Ines asked cautiously.

I hesitated a little too long.

"Preston?" She drew out my name.

"You can't tell Brody."

"Tell Brody what?" she nearly screeched.

Damn me and my big mouth. I sighed. "I met with Felipe at this club two nights ago. We set up a deal, and now I'm just waiting for him to call me with the time and place."

"Are you in-fucking-sane?" Ines yelled, and I winced. "Your brother is going to kill you. When were you going to tell him? What happens if you get caught and arrested? Or worse, what if he suggests you sample the product? Did you think about that? Oh my god."

"This isn't the cartel, Ines. You don't 'sample the product'. You buy it and walk away. I was going to tell Brody once it had been confirmed. I'd planned on having him close as backup. I'm not stupid."

"Are you sure?" she snapped. "Because setting up a drug deal sounds pretty stupid to me. Did you even think about how Brody would feel knowing that you just put yourself in a potentially dangerous situation? I can't believe what you were thinking. Never mind, because it's obvious you weren't."

Damn, she was really pissed. "Fine, I'll tell my brother as soon as he walks in the door. Will that make you happy?"

She huffed. "None of this makes me happy."

"I know it doesn't. But I'm going to tell you the same thing I told Brody." I paused, hoping she'd sense how important this was. "You have to trust me."

Ines was quiet on the other end. Finally, she replied. "I do trust you. I just can't help but worry. About both of you."

"I know you do. I love you for it, too."

"I don't want anything to come between you and your brother again. He's miserable when you guys fight. You know how he is. He wants to save everyone."

Wasn't that the truth. "Yes, I know. But, Ines…sometimes we have to save ourselves."

The office door swung open, and Brody stepped through, holding a cup in one hand while gripping the edge of another in between his teeth.

I spoke into the phone. "I gotta go. I'll talk to you soon."

My brother shut the door behind him and grabbed the

cup from between his teeth and set the one he'd been holding on my desk. "Hot cocoa."

"Thanks."

"Who was that?" he gestured toward the phone with his chin.

"Huh? Oh, that was Ines."

Brody carefully sat down in his rickety chair. "Did she find anything out from Pablo then?"

Damn it. I rubbed my hand over my face and braced myself for my brother's rage. "Nothing I didn't already find out on my own. Which,"—I paused a minute, stalling for time—"we should probably talk about."

He slowly lowered his coffee cup. "I'm not sure I like the sound of that."

I snorted. "Yeah, that's probably an understatement."

Brody's eyes narrowed. "What's going on, Preston?"

"I have a possible lead on *Rapture*. Sometime soon, I'm going to get a phone call from a guy named Cruz. He works for our suspected dealer, Felipe. We're setting up a day and time for an exchange to be made. Once it's made, and we get confirmation that he's our guy, we can start tailing them both. Find out where they live. Figure out where they go. Who they're talking to. See if we can get a lead on his supplier. Isn't that what PIs do?"

There it was, my entire plan all laid out. It seemed simple in my head, but now that I'd said it out loud it, it sounded a lot more complicated. There were so many parts of the equation that needed to align perfectly. So many things that could go wrong. One wrong move and everything would be fucked. *Shit, Ines was right. So stupid of me.*

My brother continued staring at me, and I resisted the

urge to fidget. Instead, I straightened and stared right back, almost daring him to challenge me.

"Okay, so let's say this Felipe isn't the one dealing *Rapture*. Then what? Or what if the deal goes south? Let's say it all works perfectly, and we get a tail, but it doesn't lead us to the supplier? What do we do next?"

His calm questions freaked me out. I'd expected this massive explosion of fury. I tried to think quickly.

"If he's not the dealer we're looking for, then we keep looking. If I think I'm in trouble, then I call for backup." I couldn't help smiling a little, but let it drift off my face. "I'm not in this alone. I know you've got my back. Besides, there's no reason for anything to go south. It's not like I don't know how to conduct a drug deal."

"True." Brody smirked and nodded. "Keep going. What about the rest? What if we start surveillance on them, but we don't find his supplier?"

I ignored his dig. "Then I guess we're back to square one."

Brody leaned forward onto his desk. "No, we're not back to square one. Because if they make us, then your little drug dealer knows it had all been a set up. Which means he's going to be extra cautious about who he deals with. It'll be that much harder to find who we're looking for."

"I'm willing to take that risk. I think we can make this work. We already know he frequents *Club Delight*. The place is owned by Elliott King. It's also worth taking a look at him. Ines said he's clean, but I don't think there's a chance in hell that that much narcotic movement is happening at his place of business and he doesn't know about it. If it were my club, I'd most definitely be interested in what was happening inside."

My brother still hadn't yelled and raged at me for this whole Felipe thing. It was freaking me the fuck out.

"You might be onto something. We definitely need to make sure that you have some type of backup during the exchange, but I think your plan could actually work."

Had I fallen asleep at my desk and was dreaming this whole time? Because this was not the brother I expected to get.

"Wait, I'm confused."

"About what?"

I gestured with my hands. "All of this. I went to a bar *by myself*, met a random drug dealer, and set up an exchange without telling you. You seem, oh, I don't know...okay with it? I mean, even Ines yelled at me."

Brody laughed. "Do you *want me* to yell at you?"

I stared at him wide-eyed and shook my head. "Uh, no."

"Look. I told you I trusted you. It may not have been the smartest thing you've ever done, but it doesn't matter. You may actually be the only one who can get us close to this. You've been on the streets. Have firsthand knowledge how deals like this take place. I don't mean this the way it's going to come out, but you're one of them."

I sat back in disbelief. All this time, a part of me had been worried that Brody wasn't going to trust me. I'd been preparing myself for it, in fact. But this. I'd never expected this.

"I don't know what to say," I breathed out.

"Look, I'll admit I'm not excited about this whole plan of yours, and I'm definitely annoyed that you did it behind my back. But I think it's smart. Like you said, it's a risk. But definitely one I think is worth taking."

"Thank you. This means a lot to me."

"We'll need to talk to Landon. Probably even the Rodriguez brothers. Get them up to speed on what's going on. Manuel can work on getting you mic'd. Pablo—"

"No," I interrupted. "No mics."

"Preston."

"It's not happening. That's how people like me get killed. No fucking way. I guarantee Felipe and his buddy Cruz will be checking me for a wire. That I can't risk."

"How do you expect us to make sure you stay safe if we can't hear what's going on?"

"We'll figure something out. A hand gesture or signal of some kind if I think things are going bad. But I'm not wearing a goddamn mic."

"Stubborn bastard."

"That may be so, but that's the way this is going to work."

Brody sat there, glaring at me, but I didn't budge.

"Fuck," he growled. "We'll do it your way this time. But if at any time I feel something isn't right, we're coming in and stopping it. Even if we lose Felipe and any lead we might get."

I inclined my head, stopping while I was ahead. "That's fine. In the meantime, I think we need to start taking a little closer look at Mr. King. Check his financials. Look at his businesses. It's also possible that if he does have a stake in this whole thing, then not everything he owns will be transparent."

Brody grabbed paper and pen and started taking notes. "He'd need to have a location big enough to not only store his supply, but also be able to cut it. I'm going to call Landon again and see if she was able to get the chemical analysis report. Find out what the cutting agent is. I think that's behind the overdoses. We also need to try and find out how many players are in this game."

That was the big unknown. "Right now we've got Felipe and Cruz. If King is involved, which I highly suspect, are they working directly with him, or is there yet another middle man? My guess is, there's at least one more person in between," I speculated. "There's no way whoever is in charge of this is going to be the direct contact with those who are selling it. He'd want some level of separation between them and him. Those two may not even know who's at the top. Which means extra work for us. I knew this wasn't going to be that easy."

"Let's just take one step at a time," Brody cautioned. "We need to figure out if Felipe and Cruz are even our guys. Then we can figure out where they're getting the stuff from and worry about connecting the dots later."

"Okay," I agreed. "I'll reach out to the everyone and let them know what's going on. We need to start thinking about the next stage of the plan now, as well as a plan for any contingencies that might come up."

Brody nodded. "I agree. Set up a meeting here tomorrow if you can. I'll start working on King. See what I can start finding out about his possible connection to all this."

I saluted him. "You got it."

I'd give Victor a call, but I planned on having a face-to-face with Landon. It was time for us to talk.

CHAPTER 13

I HADN'T BEEN HOME ten minutes before the knock came. Who the hell was that? Barely missing tripping over the damn cat, I hustled to the front door and peeked through the blinds. *Son of a bitch.* Glancing around the place, I spotted all the dust on the TV stand and the sink full of dirty dishes. I jerked the door open. "What are you doing here? Did you follow me? Again? For god's sake, Preston, you have to stop doing that."

He smiled, unrepentantly. It sent a hum straight to my core. Damn him. "It's really cold out here. You gonna let me in or leave me out here to freeze to death?"

I harrumphed. "I should leave your sorry ass out there. It would serve you right for showing up announced. How did you even know where I lived?"

He shrugged. "Like you said, I followed you. I didn't know how else to find you, and I'm pretty sure you didn't want me showing up at your office. Now, let me in before my nuts freeze off."

Stepping back, I opened the door wider for Preston to

enter. His spring-and-sunshine scent followed in his wake as he moved past me. Briefly, I closed my eyes and inhaled the fragrance. God, I'd missed that smell even as I hated it. I quickly shut the door behind me, and pressed back against it, trying to calm my racing heart. He stood far too close.

Preston pulled off his beanie and stuck it in his coat pocket before smoothing his hair down. A smile threatened at the sight of the few strands he missed that hovered over his head from static electricity. I smothered it. "Couldn't you have just called?"

"Didn't have your number."

Without asking, he toed off his shoes, leaving them on the linoleum next to the coat closet and then shrugged out of his coat, hanging it on the doorknob.

"Sure, just make yourself at home," I huffed, crossing my arms.

He glanced over his shoulder at me as he stepped further into the living room. "Thanks."

Just then, Sherbert made an appearance, head butting Preston's leg. "Well, hey there." Without pause, he reached down and picked up the orange tabby. I could only stare. That cat *hated* anyone besides me touching him. He'd growl at whoever tried to pick him up. And here that little shit was, sitting, happy as a clam in Preston's arms, purring so loud I could hear him from over here. *Traitorous asshole.*

The two of them walked around the room, the human whispering nonsense in the damn cat's ear. His eyes darted up to meet mine, and he went back to talking in the feline's ear. *He wasn't talking about me, was he?* I shook my head. *No, that's ridiculous.*

"Why are you here, Preston? And don't say it's because you followed me. I want to know *why* you followed me."

"I told you we were going to talk."

He was right. He'd warned me, but I kept thinking he was just going to let it go. I should have known better. I didn't know what I was going to say. Nothing had changed. "Fine. Let's talk." I just wanted to get it over with.

"Do you mind if I sit?"

I almost laughed. Now he wanted to be polite and ask? I gestured to the couch. "Have a seat. Wanna beer?" Might as well be hospitable.

"No, thanks. I don't drink. Well, usually. I've actually only had one drink in the last two years."

I didn't even think about him being in recovery. "Yeah, sorry. I forgot. I have water if you'd rather."

He shook his head, settling on the end of the couch with Sherbert in his lap. "I'm fine, thanks."

I sat on the far opposite end of the sofa from Preston, who smiled. "Scared?"

My eyes narrowed. "No."

"So, I went to *Club Delight*."

"Yes, I remember. I was there."

His attention remained on the cat. "No, I mean, later that night. Without you."

I reared back. "What?"

"You didn't get the answers either of us needed, so I thought I'd try my luck."

"And?"

"I met Felipe and his buddy Cruz. Lovely fellas." I heard his sarcasm. "And before you yell at me for being stupid, believe me when I tell you that Ines has already beaten you to it."

"Why would I yell? Or tell you you were being stupid?"

"Because I arranged a drug deal while I was there."

I sat for a moment trying to puzzle out what the problem was. "Okay, I think you need to explain things to me, because I'm not sure how that makes you stupid. We're trying to track down the dealer of this *Rapture.* You seem to have found him and you set up an exchange. I assume you're planned on having backup during this little deal, correct?"

Preston stared at me like I was crazy, his brow creased. "Yeah, that was my plan."

"Great. So when and where is this business transaction happening?"

He held his palm toward me. "Hold on a minute. I'm trying to process this."

I had no idea what he needed to process. I couldn't keep quiet any longer though. "I still think I'm missing something."

He chuckled. "Ines was beyond pissed off. According to her, it was completely irresponsible of me. She was concerned that I'd gotten into a bad situation. That this could cause me to relapse."

My eyes widened as it finally hit me. "Ohhhh."

"Yeah."

It hadn't really hit me that this could be a problem. I couldn't help but study him. Maybe Ines knew Preston better than I did. I mean, how well *did* I really know him?

"Do *you* think you're going to relapse?" I asked.

Preston paused long enough to make me nervous.

"I'm an addict. Always will be," he finally said. "Our client handed me that empty baggie of *Rapture,* and just the smell alone made my palms sweat and my body ache for a single taste. It was like being reunited with an old friend. Staying clean is the hardest thing I've ever had to do."

"So, is that a yes?"

His eyes met mine. "There's always that chance."

From the moment I'd seen the marks on his arms, I'd always been curious. "Do you mind if I ask what got you started on drugs? You don't have to answer. I know it's a pretty personal question."

Sherbert must have decided he'd had enough cuddling time, because he jumped down and strolled across the living room, to plop in a spot of sun that filtered through the kitchen window. I turned back to Preston.

"No, it's fine. I can understand why you'd wonder." He paused and took a deep breath. "You probably know that Brody is ten years older than me."

I nodded.

"He and I were always close despite our age difference. He practically raised me, since our mom worked two jobs. She was a single parent with two kids. Of course, Brody helped out once he turned sixteen. But then he went off to college. It had always been the two of us. And then, it was just me."

The faraway look in his eye kept me quiet. I didn't want to disturb him. He continued. "It was my friend's sixteenth birthday. Some guy threw him a party. His parents had gone out of town, so the house was empty. We were teenagers. We raided the fridge and cracked open some beers. I think I'd had one, maybe two. The next thing I know, the guy throwing the party pulled out a small baggie. I figured one time wouldn't hurt, right?" Preston laughed, but it wasn't because the story was funny. He shook his head. "One time turned into a lot of times. And then coke turned into heroin. I had to feed that rush, you know?"

I didn't know what to say. Instead, I scooted closer and

reached out to lay my hand on his. He jerked at my touch, he was so lost in the past. His eyes darted down to our hands. He turned his over and threaded our fingers.

"When did you get clean?" I whispered.

"Which time? There's been so many."

"The first time."

Preston swallowed, but didn't answer. I waited. Then he let my hand go and rose from the couch. He strode across the room and stood near my mantle, refusing to look at me. Still I remained quiet. I didn't want to push him.

"Did Brody ever tell you why he joined the D.E.A.?"

I blinked in surprise, not sure where he was going with the question. "I assumed he joined for the same reason we all did. It was a place where we could do some good."

"By the time I'd turned seventeen, I'd already gone from coke to heroin. Which is a lot more expensive. One day, I was high, and freaked out because my stash was nearly empty. I needed more, but I didn't have any money. I couldn't hold a job, even though I'd tried." He stopped a moment. "I don't have firsthand memory of the rest of this. I only know what Brody told me. I'd come home, frantic, rummaging through my mom's purse looking for some cash. She saw what I was doing and tried to stop me. We wrestled over her purse. She lost her grip and fell. I grabbed all the money I could out of her wallet and took off."

I tried covering my gasp with my fingers. "Oh my god." The words came out muffled behind them.

"She hit her head and ruptured an aneurysm in her brain. She was dead in seconds."

It all made sense. His scars. The need for atonement. For forgiveness.

I rose from the couch, stopping just short of him. My

fingers tingled with the need to touch him. Our night together came to mind. Preston had taken my pain away. It was only fair that I try to do the same for him. Pushing aside the fear that kept holding me back, I wrapped my arms around his waist and laid my head against his back, trying to offer him the same comfort he'd given me.

"That's why you're doing all this, isn't it? You're trying to make up for your sins."

He flinched, and then relaxed. "Yes."

"I admire you. Your strength," I whispered almost against my will.

It was true. Preston didn't seem to let anything stop him or hold him back from getting what he wanted. Which terrified me down to my soul. Because he hadn't made any secret of the fact that he wanted me. Someone who didn't deserve him. Or deserve to be loved. Not after what I'd done. That sharp reminder had me pulling away.

He turned to face me. "Why do you do that?"

I wrapped my arms around myself. "Do what?"

"That. Put distance between us. Run. I can see you fighting against yourself. You admitted that night that you felt the connection between us, but now you deny it existed. No matter what I say or do, you keep running." He tried closing the distance between us, and I unconsciously took a small step back. "Just like that. What are you afraid of?"

He didn't understand. "It has nothing to do with being afraid."

"Then what does it have to do with? *Your* sins? Have you still not forgiven yourself for them?"

I flinched at the question, and bit back all the things I wanted to say to him. We stared at each other, neither giving an inch, until finally, Preston was the first to look away. He moved around me and headed toward the front.

"Brody wants everyone to come to the office tomorrow afternoon around four so we can try to come up with several different plans and scenarios for when this deal goes down. I guess I'll see you there."

I watched him put his shoes back on and grab his coat. He shrugged into it and turned back toward me, his eyes boring into mine, like he was begging for me to ask him to stay. I couldn't.

It wasn't fair to him, and I cared too much about him to hurt him that way. His shoulders sagged in defeat.

"I miss Sara. At least *she* wasn't a coward." And then he was gone, leaving me alone, even though my heart was calling for him to come back.

CHAPTER 14

I PULLED into the driveway of the small, bright yellow bungalow style ranch with white shutters and parked next to a dark blue pickup truck. Snow covered the entire yard, and the poor flower bed along the porch border was full of shriveled up bushes.

The sidewalk had been shoveled, but I still kicked off the bits of snow clinging to my shoes. I knocked on the front door, shoving my free hand in my pocket to try and warm it while I waited for someone to answer. Finally, it opened.

"Hey, man." Victor stepped back and let me in. I bumped my shoulder against his with a single thump on his back in greeting.

"Thanks for meeting me for lunch." I held up the bag in my hand. "I brought us a couple burgers and steak fries."

"Sounds good. Let me take it and you can hang your coat in the closet."

Victor headed into the kitchen, and I met him in there.

"Not that I don't want to hang out with you, but what's going on that we needed to have lunch together? Pablo and I are heading to your office at four." He distributed the food he'd pulled out of the bag.

Besides Brody, Victor was my only friend. I really needed to talk to someone, and since this involved Landon, it had to be someone besides my brother.

"I'm invoking the bro code," I started.

"What the hell is the bro code?"

"It means that this is just between us. You can't tell Estelle. And you definitely can't tell Brody."

"Is this about anything illegal?"

"What?" My head jerked back. "No."

Victor held his hands up. "I was just checking. I mean, I didn't plan on telling Brody either way, but I was really kind of hoping for something illegal."

I chuckled and shook my head. "You're an asshole."

He grinned. "Anyway, what's this big secret I can't tell anyone?"

Now that the opportunity to get things off my chest was here, I hesitated. The only people I'd really ever told my problems to were my sponsor and my therapists every time I landed in rehab. Did guys actually even talk about this kind of shit with each other?

At my silence, Victor wiped the grin off his face. "Seriously, what's going on?"

"Landon and I slept together," I blurted out.

His eyes bulged. "I'm sorry, what?"

"It was two years ago. Neither of us knew who the other was. She even gave me a fake name. I was having a rough day, and based on all the drinking she was doing that night, so was she. One thing led to another. She was gone before I woke up, and I didn't see her again until outside Álvarez's warehouse over two months ago."

"Holy shit," he choked out. "No wonder you don't want Brody to know. Have you guys hooked up again since then?"

My laugh was bitter. "Not even close. She keeps denying there was something between us. That there's *still* something between us."

"Oh, man," Victor commiserated sympathetically. "I know what you're going through. Estelle fought me every step of the way. She was worth the fight though."

"Landon is, too. But, god, she's so frustrating." I dropped my head and rubbed the back of my neck trying to ease the tension out of it. I blew out a long breath. "That's not even the worst of it."

"Hell. What could be worse?"

"I haven't been sleeping much. Too many dreams. Some are about her. About that night." Shame settled deep in my gut. Just admitting to the next made me feel weak. Yesterday Landon had called me strong. She didn't know the truth. I wasn't strong. Not even close. "Most of all, I dream about getting high."

"Oh, fuck," Victor whispered.

My gaze met his worried one. "Yeah, fuck. I haven't had that particular dream since my last relapse. That's always how it used to go down though. I'd go to sleep and dream about being high. Soon after that, I'd make the dream a reality. I refuse to let that happen again. Not this time."

"What are you going to do?"

That's what I kept asking myself. My life was different now. I had my brother back. I had Ines, Victor, and the rest of their family. I had a job I loved. And then there was Landon. I didn't have her, but fuck if I didn't want to. None of that answered the question.

"I don't really know."

"What about your sponsor? Or your NA meetings?"

"I've been going to them more frequently. My sponsor hasn't really been available, although it's not her fault. She's been having a lot of serious health issues. I've called a couple of the people she's recommended, but I just haven't been able to develop a relationship with them. Which is why I'm talking to you."

Victor paced, running his hands through his hair.

"Look, I know it's a lot. But...I don't really have any other friends besides you and my brother. He'll only worry if I tell him about the dream."

"Should *I* be worried?"

"No," I said confidently, despite the fact that he probably should be. But adding Victor's worries on top of my own would only make things worse. "I'll be okay. Just knowing I have my brother, Ines, and you are enough."

I glanced down at my cold burger, my appetite gone entirely.

"Well, I'm always here for you. No matter what." Victor smiled, though it wasn't his normal one. "I'll even arrest you if you ask me to."

He was trying to cheer me up, but man, I really hope it didn't come to that. "Thanks for the advice. And for listening. I'm not really hungry anymore."

I headed back out to the living room to get my coat. "See you at four, then?"

Victor nodded. "I'll be there."

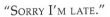

"Sorry I'm late."

I looked up to see Landon step through the office door. She glanced briefly in my direction before quickly darted her gaze toward Brody. It was quarter after four, and I'd assumed she wasn't coming. Especially after how we'd left things yesterday. Or, rather, how I'd left things.

"You're fine. We were just getting started," Brody said. "We saved you a seat."

She took the chair opposite his desk. My eyes stayed locked on her, but she continued not meeting my stare.

"I'm still trying to figure out why I'm here," Victor spoke up.

"You and your brother are the only two who actually have jurisdiction to arrest these guys if it happens to come to that."

"So how are we supposed to plan if we don't even know where the exchange is taking place? There are logistics we need to figure out. Things like where we're going to be stationed for optimal visual. Manuel should be here too. He's the one in charge of wiring people."

Brody coughed. "There won't be any wires."

Landon's head whipped in my direction. "What do you mean there won't be a wire?"

"Exactly that. All we're there to do is confirm whether or not Felipe is selling *Rapture*. You put a wire on me, I'm a dead man."

"But what if something happens? We can't be prepared if we can't hear what's going on."

"Like I told my brother, I'm willing to take that risk. Besides, I trust you to have my back."

I trusted all of them, but Landon needed to know she was the one I was talking to.

"We need to come up with multiple plans." Brody spoke.

"We don't know how these guys deal. Are we going to be in some back alley behind *Club Delight*, or will they have Preston come to a drug house?"

Pablo spoke up. "If we're lucky, it'll be somewhere near the club. All the arrests we've made that involve *Rapture* have been close by. Although none of them have involved this Felipe and Cruz, I'm going to bet that while they're in the club, they pass the drug off to someone that works for them. That person is the one that makes the exchange."

"If that's the case, then this isn't going to work. We have to make it happen with Felipe and Cruz. Otherwise, there's no point." I shake my head.

"That's going to be something you'll have to negotiate with them when they call."

"I plan on it."

"Here's the trickier part. If they send you to a drug house we can't follow you or station ourselves in the area. That option is a lot more dangerous."

"This is all insane." Landon rose and stared down at Brody. "You're seriously going to let your brother go into a drug deal with no wire and just us as backup?"

"I trust him to know what he's doing."

Her eyes latched onto mine. "I don't think I can be a part of this."

She spun and disappeared out the office door. Brody started to rise, but I waved him down. "Let me talk to her."

He gave me a look I couldn't interpret but settled back down.

"You guys work out the logistics of where the most logical places the exchange might take place near the club, okay?"

"Will do," Victor called out. I was already halfway out the door.

I rushed down the hallway, trying to catch her before she got away. I spotted her at the elevator. "Landon, stop."

She whirled on me. "No, you stop. Do you have any idea what the hell you're doing? You're going to a drug deal with no wire and no protection. Of all the stupid and—"

I smothered the rest of her words with my mouth. My hands palmed her cheeks, afraid she'd pull away. With a sigh, she wound her arms around my waist and clutched me tightly to her as our tongues battled for control. Then she jerked her mouth from mine and stared up at me as we both tried to catch our breath. I brushed the hair out of her eyes. The light behind her cast a halo around her head, giving her the appearance of an angel. If she was an angel, then I was the devil.

"You have to trust me to know what I'm doing. This isn't the first time I've done this sort of thing, you know." I smiled sarcastically. "I've been buying drugs for over a decade."

She punched me in the arm. "It's not funny."

My smile disappeared. "I'm not trying to be. I'm glad you're worried about me."

There was a cough behind us, and I spun around, both of us dropping our hands to our sides.

"Just came out here to check on the two of you." Victor stood there with a huge smile on his face. "Looks like you were doing just fine."

I chuckled, and Landon smacked my arm again. "Tell Brody we're on our way."

"You got it, my friend."

Victor disappeared down the hallway, and I turned back to Landon who stood there with her arms crossed.

"He didn't seem too surprised to see you kissing me."

I mimicked her pose. "I'm pretty sure you were the one doing the kissing. And no, he wasn't surprised."

"So, he knows about us?"

"I thought there wasn't an us."

"You know what I mean."

"To answer your question, yes, he knows."

"What did you tell him?"

I let out a sigh and lowered my arms. "I told him we met a couple years ago and hadn't seen each other since then. What should I have told him?"

Landon's whole body seemed to collapse in exhaustion. She backed away a few steps. "I don't know."

We needed to get back in the office before Brody came out to check on us next. "Come on. Let's go back inside and figure out our plan. We'll worry about other things later."

She met my gaze. "Fine."

I led her back to the office where everyone waited. Two sets of eyes studied us. I didn't meet Victor's knowing stare.

"You guys okay?" Brody asked.

It took me a second to understand his question. "Yeah, we're fine. Talked things out."

Victor coughed.

"I'm reluctantly on board with the plan," Landon acknowledged.

"Great. Now that we have that settled, here's what Pablo and I came up with so far."

An hour later we had several contingency plans in place. The only thing left to do was wait for the call from Cruz. He should have called by now. Which was making me a little nervous.

Brody spoke up. "I know this might seem like overkill for

such a simple deal, but I'd rather not take any chances. All Preston has to do is get in, get the confirmation we need, and get out. We're not there to make an arrest. Not yet anyway. Not unless we absolutely have to. It's information only. Then Preston and I plan on doing surveillance. See if we can't find their supplier."

"We appreciate everyone's help on this," I added.

"No problem. You guys are family now. We'll always have your back." Victor clasped my hand and pulled me in for a chest bump.

Pablo shook my hand. Then the two brothers left, with Landon right behind them after she said a quick goodbye. My eyes lingered on her until she was out of sight. I turned back to find Brody staring at me.

"What?" I ignored his speculative glare and sat down at my desk to pull out a file from my drawer.

"I feel like something's going on, but I can't figure out what it is."

This wasn't good. Brody loved puzzles. If there was something he couldn't figure out, then he didn't let it go until he did. Which meant I needed to solve it for him.

"I was admiring the view. I can't help it that Landon's hot." I shrugged. "Is she single?"

My brother's expression quickly shifted to horrified. "No fucking way. She could be the last woman on this earth, and there's no way anything would happen between you two."

I tried my best to look offended, although it didn't take much. "Why not? We're about the same age. I have a good-paying job. I shower every day. I'm a decent looking guy. I'm quite the catch if you ask me."

"No one asked you. I don't even want to picture the two of you together." Brody shuddered.

"You should see your face. Don't worry, just because I think she's hot doesn't mean I have any interest in her beyond that. God, could you imagine? A D.E.A. agent and a recovering heroin addict. I'm sure that would go over well." I laughed, but the image wouldn't leave my head.

Brody chuckled and went back to his computer. "Jesus. That would be a disaster."

I smothered my laughter into a strained smile and opened the file I still held in my hand. I stared at the information inside, but not seeing any of it. I kept hearing my brother's words over and over.

CHAPTER 15

IT HAD BEEN hours since I'd left Preston and Brody's office, and I could still almost feel the imprint of his lips on mine. He tasted exactly the same as he had two years ago. His unique flavor continued to linger in my mouth. I stroked Sherbert's back, lost in the memories of that night and all the lonely nights since then.

Coward.

Coward.

Preston's accusation kept ringing in my ear. It hadn't stopped since yesterday. I wiped away a stupid stray tear.

For nineteen years I hadn't shed a single one. Until that night with Preston. Ever since then, I shed them far too often, as though making up for lost time. I hated them. They made me feel weak. God, he was right. I was such a coward. I couldn't think of that right now. I also didn't need to think about all the things that could go wrong with this stupid drug deal he'd set up. Whoever was behind this drug was dangerous. Especially considering how much money they would lose if they were caught. Millions and millions of dollars.

I could still feel Preston's penetrating gaze when he said he trusted me. He'd been addressing all of us, but he'd been looking straight at me. Telling me, personally, that it was me he trusted. Why though? I hadn't given him a single reason to.

I refused to let him down.

The doorbell ringing startled me. I glanced at the clock. Only one person would show up at my house this late. My heart started racing. Setting down the bottle of beer I'd been nursing, I lifted Sherbert off my lap, planted him on the couch, and rose. I took several deep breaths before finally letting him in. My eyes looked him over from head to toe, and then I stepped back so he could enter. Deja vu swept over me as Preston toed off his shoes and hung his coat on the doorknob of the coat closet. I closed the front door and pressed myself against it, while he wandered into the living room to once again pick up Sherbert, who let him.

"I wondered if you would stop by after that kiss."

He turned at my words. "I wondered if you'd let me through the door."

Of course I was going to. "You were right. I am a coward."

Even in the dim light, I could see the hue of his cheeks darken and shame flash across his face.

"I shouldn't have said that. It was wrong of me, and I'm sorry."

"No." I stepped toward him. "No. You were absolutely right. I have been running from you. Ever since that morning. I haven't stopped."

"Why?" he asked for at least the hundredth time. That

had always been the one thing he'd wanted to know. I couldn't give him the entire answer he was asking for, but I could at least give him part of it.

"Sit." I gestured to the couch. "Please."

Preston set Sherbert on the floor and took a seat. I followed behind, still keeping a short distance between us. I tried to gather my thoughts.

"I love snow. Always have. When I was little, I actually wanted to live inside a snow globe." I snorted at how ridiculous that sounded. "It seemed like the most beautiful place to be with all that snow floating around, all glittery and sparkly and magical. That's what that night was. Like I was in my own personal snow globe. But come morning, once I was awake, all that snow had settled, and it wasn't that pretty, sparkly, magical place where everything was perfect. Real life intruded. Real life is ugly. Harsh. Brutal."

"I don't agree with you."

My head swiveled, and I met Preston's eyes.

"Real life isn't always ugly. It can also be beautiful. I don't think you have to live inside some snow globe to experience magic. You can find it anywhere, even the real world, if you only look hard enough."

He scooted closer to me, and my breath caught in my chest. His hand palmed the back of my neck. "Take right now, for instance. I'm looking at you, and I see all things beautiful and magical."

Was that really how he saw me? I looked in the mirror and saw pain. Loneliness. Sometimes death. It was hard to see beauty in any of those things.

"Let me show you what I see when I look at you." Preston brushed a kiss across my cheek. "Kindness." Another kiss across my forehead. "Intelligence." Yet another one on the tip of my nose. "Stubbornness." My eyelids drifted shut, and there was a soft touch over each one. "Loyalty."

His breath hovered over my lips, and I had to hold myself back from leaning forward to touch mine to his. I waited for the feel of his mouth, but it didn't come. My eyes shot open and met his gaze. Then he ever so slowly lowered his head that final inch. "Courage."

Preston pulled back, but his face had become a blur. His thumb brushed across my cheek smearing wetness across it.

"I see *you*, Landon."

I wanted to be all those things he saw. To *deserve* to be all those things. Especially courageous. I wanted that more than anything.

With a racing heart, I rose from the couch to stare down at this man who saw something in me that I couldn't see in myself.

I held out a hand that trembled. His sparkling eyes stared up at me and then, with an aching slowness, he laid his warm fingers against mine and stood. My eyes followed the movement until I was staring up at him. He was so close, the heat of his body seeped into mine and his scent surrounded us. I raised our hands and pressed his palm to my cheek. A spark ignited against my lips and traveled through me until it landed straight in my core. I turned my head to press a kiss to his skin.

Two years ago, I'd needed Preston to take my pain away. Tonight, I just needed him. Only this time, I didn't ask.

"Come to my room."

His eyes heated and his nostrils flared. Still holding his hand, I pivoted and pulled him along behind me, leading him down the hall and into my bedroom. To my surprise, he turned the light switch on.

"I want to see it all this time."

A tremor skittered across my skin. No shadows to hide behind. He could look into my eyes and see all my emotion, because there was no way I was going to be able to lock them away. If his intent was to make me feel even more vulnerable than I already did, he'd succeeded. I wasn't backing away from his challenge, whether intentional or not. I wouldn't always compare being together with that first night... *did that mean there was going to be a next time?* I shook off the thought.

The last time, he'd allowed me privacy, and I'd quickly disrobed and scurried under the covers like a scared mouse. Not tonight. Taking two steps back, trying to draw on the courage Preston seemed to think I possessed, I tugged my shirt up and over my head. His gaze dropped to my chest before quickly returning to meet my eyes. A slow half-smile appeared on his face. Boldly, I reached behind and unhooked my bra before pulling the straps down and discarding it to lie on the floor on top of my shirt. If I thought the heat in his eyes had been bright before, nothing compared to the firestorm that shone from them.

A rush of power I didn't know I possessed surged through me that I could affect him that much. It was a heady feeling. My pants and underwear followed until I stood completely naked. My nipples were hard and my breasts actually ached, whether from the cold or from a fierce need to have the touch of his strong fingers on them. I closed the distance between us and without hesitation I rose on tiptoe, my hands splayed against his chest for balance, to press my lips to his. His sharp inhalation gave me the opening I wanted to dart my tongue in for a taste. I flicked it against his, teasing, chasing, drawing him into the game. He answered my challenge.

The skin on my lower back burned from the touch of his palms against it. My core throbbed in time to my racing pulse. I ground my pelvis against the hard ridge of his cock, wanting the friction. My frantic movements ignited a need inside Preston and what started out as a simple kiss turned explosive.

He speared a hand through my hair, holding tight, to give him the leverage he needed to tilt my head and deepen the kiss. His tongue was no longer playful. Instead, the power behind his kiss made my legs tremble, and if not for his strong arms holding me tightly, I may have crumbled. But no way was he letting me fall. I was right where he'd been fighting to get me this last month. At his mercy.

Breathless, he pulled back to stare at me, his eyes nearly losing all the brown, and into a forest green.

"What do you want, Landon?"

My forehead crinkled. I wasn't sure what he was asking me.

"Two years ago, you wanted me to take your pain away. What do you want now?"

The confusion cleared. As though he'd read my mind, he wanted me to acknowledge that there was more to this need I had for him. If that was what he wanted, I would give it to him.

"Only you."

After the words were out, I stared deep into his eyes so he could read the truth in mine. His expression shifted to one of determination. Keeping a tight grip on me, Preston walked me backwards until the back of my knees hit the bed. He released me, and with a gentle push they buckled and my butt hit the mattress. I tilted my head back to keep my eyes locked on his.

"You have me. Which also means I have you. They go hand in hand, so you better be sure."

His words of warning made me nervous and the hairs on my neck stood at attention. Pushing them aside for now, I drew on some newly discovered confidence and reached out to undo his jeans before sliding them down his legs. His erection jutted out through his boxer briefs. I slid my fingers along the elastic band, grazing his stomach, and he sucked in his breath with a hiss. I tugged those down as well and his hard cock bobbed, the purplish head gleaming with a drop of wetness. He gripped the bottom of his shirt and pulled it up over his head before stepping one foot out of his pants and kicking them away with the other. His shirt was tossed away.

I scooted backward up to the head of the bed, and like a predator spotting his prey, he set a knee on the bed and stalked toward me, his body separating my legs so he could settle in between them. I'd seen the ink across his chest and arms before, but not like this. My eyes landed on the name on his right pec. My fingers traced it, and he flinched.

"Is that your mother?"

"Yes," he answered in the gravelly voice of his.

"I'm sorry."

He shrugged, but I saw the pain in his eyes and heard it in his voice. "It was a long time ago."

"Time doesn't make the ache go away. It's always there, hovering just below the surface, poking and prodding at us as though trying to keep the memory fresh and the pain constant."

"Yeah, that's exactly what it's like."

I leaned up and pressed a light kiss to the tattoo before lying back. Preston's arms caged my head, and he dipped down to crush his lips to mine. He took control, lashing his tongue against mine before nipping my bottom lip and then moving down. He nibbled and sucked his way to both breasts, pulling each hardened tip into the hot cavern of his mouth, gently grinding his teeth around my turgid nipple.

Pleasure shot through me and my thighs were slick with wetness that shot from me with the tiny bit of pain his bite caused. I cried out at the feel of his fingers gathering my juice and circling my clit matching the movements of his tongue around my breast. Pressure was building deep inside me and my clit throbbed and tingled, the nerves sparking pleasure. With a few flicks of his thumb, my body couldn't contain the sensations. My body thrashed, the orgasm ripped through me faster than I expected. Preston didn't let up, he only rubbed harder sending more shockwaves through me until I gasped and screamed through a second. He pulled his fingers away, and before I could catch my breath, he thrust home.

He didn't move, merely let me get used to the feel of him. My muscles clenched down, and he groaned, shifting a little, which sent a tiny spasm through me. He raised his head and our eyes met in the brightness of the room. I was far too tired to put on the mask I always tried to wear. Every emotion was laid bare for him to witness. I showed him all my fears. Judging by the fierce glow in his eyes, he would soothe all of them away. The defenses I'd built around my heart, for nearly my entire life, cracked just a little. I tried not to jerk at the pinch of unease it brought.

Even though Preston had given me two orgasms already,

my body was still buzzing. His throbbing cock continued to keep me on edge. My fingers gripped his arms tightly. *Courage.*

"Make love to me," I said, my voice strong and sure.

As though that was all he'd been waiting for, he began to move. Slowly at first, but gaining strength, until his thrusts became punishing. My legs circled his waist, and I latched my ankles together.

"Harder," I begged, my words choked.

I sucked in a breath as he did just that. There was an edge of pain to the pleasure, and I wanted more of it. It hurt so good and soon that same throbbing tension built. Preston changed angles and with each powerful thrust, he scraped across my clit. It only took a few more hard pushes and my nails dragged down his back as ecstasy soared through me once again. I bit down on his shoulder, smothering my scream. He increased his pace and then his roar echoed in my ear and the warm splash of his seed filled me up.

My whole body trembled. I managed to untangle my legs from around him, and Preston collapsed onto his back, his harsh breathing matching mine. He turned his head toward me and just watched me without a word. I swallowed the lump forming in my throat. *Courage.*

Our breaths slowed and a shiver ghosted across my skin in the cold air. Preston pulled the covers over us but didn't get up to shut off the light.

Apparently my courage only extended so far, because I couldn't put into words what I was feeling. So I stayed quiet. He glanced at me again, and his eyes had lost their bright, fiery sheen. *Was I disappointing him?* Probably, but I was nearly drowning in new and fucking scary emotions. They were too fresh. I hoped he'd understand why I just...couldn't.

He sighed and then pulled me against his chest, tucking me under his shoulder. I cuddled closer and laid my hand directly over his heart. It was the closest I could come to showing him how I felt. Despite the bright, overhead light, the day finally caught up with me, and I closed my eyes trusting Preston to keep my nightmares away.

CHAPTER 16

A SLOW TUG of awareness brought me out of sleep. I rolled over, eyes still closed, dragging the sheet with me. The scent of lavender and vanilla came with it. *Landon.* Last night came rushing back to me. My eyes opened to find an empty bed and equally empty room. It stung, but I shouldn't have expected anything different.

I was trying to be patient. I didn't want to fuck this up by pushing her too hard. We'd had a breakthrough last night. At least it felt like one. There was so much she still held back. Then again, Landon had proved she was nothing if not stubborn.

Reluctance and need warred within me. The same compulsion that always came over me to see her made its presence known. But I was also reluctant, because it seemed like every time I saw her again, it was like I had to start all over. I'd wear her down and slowly her acceptance of me came. The longer we were together, the easier things between us were.

But the second I left, it was like she forgot and quickly

rebuilt some internal wall. I wanted to knock the damn thing down entirely, but that wasn't my decision. She needed to be the one who stopped putting it up in the first place.

As tempting as it was to stay in here and wait to see if she came to me, I couldn't. I climbed out of the bed and headed into the master bath. After splashing some water on my face, I walked back into the bedroom. My clothes lay rumpled on the floor where I'd dropped them last night. Quickly throwing them back on, I went in search of Landon.

Two familiar voices, one feminine, the other masculine, stopped me the second I stepped into the living room.

"What the *fuck*? Preston?" That was my brother.

"Shit." And that was Landon.

My gaze landed on Brody first. His expression was a combination of confusion and rage. Both, of which, I could understand. I expected them, because this thing between Landon and me wasn't going stay secret forever. No matter how I'd tried to throw him off track yesterday.

My eyes darted over to the woman in question. My heart sank at her expression. The horror and mortification I got. But that flash of…shame? That one hurt, especially after yesterday.

"One of you needs to tell me what's going on. Now," Brody bit out the word.

My gaze hadn't left Landon's. Neither of us spoke, as though daring the other to go first. I wanted to hear how she was going to explain this.

Us.

I thought last night had changed things between us. I didn't try and hide my disappointment in her the longer she stayed silent though. I blew out a huff of air and with a shake of my head, finally answered. "Apparently nothing's going on. Nothing at all."

Landon flinched at my words, but she didn't correct me. I moved past Brody to put my shoes on. Then I grabbed my coat off the closet doorknob and shrugged into it. Brody's gaze darted back and forth between the two of us like a tennis match. The room had grown heavy with tension and the thickening silence.

I took one final look at her. There wasn't anything else to say. Without waiting for my brother, I let myself out of the house, closing the door softly behind me. The bitter cold didn't even faze me. It was stupid of me to think she'd admit to anyone else whatever this was between us. Not that I had a fucking clue what it was either. There was a connection, she'd hadn't denied it. But sometimes it seemed like that wasn't enough for her.

"Preston, wait," Brody called out.

I stopped next to my car. Might as well get this over with. My scars burned under my coat. He finally reached me, but didn't say anything. Just stared at me, assessing. "Why don't we go to Mickey's and talk."

He didn't seem angry anymore. Still confused, but more curious.

I nodded. "Fine. I'll meet you there."

MICKEY'S BAR WAS A RELIC FROM OUR OLD NEIGHBORHOOD. Brody and I used to walk past it every day on our way home after he'd come pick me up from school. We'd smell the stale popcorn that would sit for hours in the vintage popcorn machine that used to be parked in the corner, but in recent times had been replaced with a jukebox.

It was dark and a little dingy inside with a few pool tables to the right of the front door. Several of them needed refelting, but the old guys playing couldn't care less about the few scattered tears here and there. They weren't sharks or playing for money. It was merely a way for them to pass the time while they had a few drinks with their buddies.

Grady, who stood behind the bar washing glasses, had been the bartender for as long as I could remember. His Fu Manchu had long gone to silver, and if he wasn't sporting a shiny bald head, his hair would probably match in color. I slid into my favorite booth in the back corner. The one where, as a kid, I'd carved my initials into the wood paneling on the wall with a pocketknife.

Within a few minutes of my arrival, Brody entered and made his way over and scooted across the tattered leather seat opposite me.

"Want to tell me what happened back there?" There was no accusation in his question.

"It's a long story. Probably not one you're going to like."

His lips pressed together, and he nodded. "I gathered that. I'd still like to know."

"A couple years ago, I was part of the construction crew making renovations on a hotel downtown. It was one of those days where the urges started to overwhelm me. I held them off as long as I could by going to the hotel bar right after my shift ended. I'd only meant to grab something to eat and maybe stay for an hour or two. I'd hoped to get them under control first."

"Why didn't you call your sponsor? Find a meeting?" he asked accusingly.

"Because I thought I could handle it myself."

"Preston." Brody sighed in obvious disappointment. Ten years of relapses showed I clearly didn't do well trying to handle it myself.

"I know. But then I saw her."

He sucked in a breath. "Landon?"

I nodded, my eyes unfocused as I pictured her that night. Blinking away the memory, I glanced back at my brother. "She was alone at the bar. Drinking. A lot. Some guy was harassing her, but I ran him off. I meant to leave then, too, but I couldn't. Instead, I stayed there for hours watching her."

Brody pinched the bridge of his nose like a headache was forming.

"I'd never seen so much pain in a person's eyes before." I sat for a moment, staring down at the table, my chest tight with emotion as I vividly recalled the agony in them. "We talked for a bit, about our sins. Our guilt."

He sucked in a sharp breath. "Did she tell you what her sins are?"

Something in the question jerked my head up. I locked gazes with him. "No, she didn't tell me." My eyes narrowed. "She's told you though, hasn't she?"

Brody didn't say anything for the longest time. "Yes."

So, she'd told my brother her secrets. The fact that she'd shared something so personal with him left a bitter taste in my mouth. "When I woke up the next morning, she was gone. Never saw her again until that day you all rescued Estelle."

"Jesus, Preston."

Neither of us spoke for several minutes until Brody broke the silence. "Considering you were coming out of her

121

bedroom bright and early in the morning, it looks like you've rekindled your...relationship."

My laugh was humorless. "I thought we had. Until you showed up. Every time I think I break through, she rebuilds the wall around her."

Brody studied me intently. "You really care about her, don't you?"

Did I? Two years ago, I'd felt this connection to her. Each time I saw her, it came back. Last night had only confirmed it. It made me want to know her. Not Sara. Sara had been someone who didn't exist. I wanted to know the *real* her. I wanted to know Landon. Was it because I cared for her? What other reason was there?

A sense of calm and peace settled through me at the answer. "Yeah, I do."

"She's not going to make it easy on you. You know that, right?"

This time my bark of laughter was genuine. "Why should she start now?"

Brody joined me before he grew serious again. "Not that I think you'd ask me to, but I won't tell you Landon's secrets. They're not mine to tell. Getting her to return your feelings is going to be hard. Believe me when I tell you that this fight you have ahead of you is going to be the hardest of your life. Maybe even harder than fighting your addiction."

I stared at my threaded fingers lying on the tabletop. "No doubt you're right."

My words were followed by the sound of my phone ringing. I glanced at the screen and then at Brody. "I don't recognize the number."

"Answer it," he says.

I swiped to answer. "Hello?"

"Well, hello, again, Preston."

"Felipe, what a pleasant surprise. I figured you'd forgotten about me by now."

Brody jerked to attention.

"Not at all. You made quite the impression the last time. For example, that bruise on Cruz's jaw from that right hook." He laughed. "He's still pretty pissed."

"Like I told you that night, nobody touches me."

"Yes, well. Anyway. I thought we could set up a little meet and greet. You know that whole supply and demand thing you were talking about? Unless you've found someone else?"

"I was running low on a few things I needed, so yeah, I had to have a chat with one of my old buddies."

He chuckled. "You must have been desperate."

"Not that desperate. He and I have been friends for almost a decade."

"Yes, well, I'm sure that perhaps now, you and I can become friends."

"Maybe. If things are as good as I've heard, you might become my new best friend. Otherwise, I might just stick with my old one. He's a fair priced businessman."

Felipe's laugh was loud and hearty. "You think I run an unfair business."

"Depends."

"Yes, well, why don't we set up a business meeting and you can let me know."

"You tell me when and where."

"How about tomorrow night? Say nine o'clock. There's a small children's park a few blocks from the club we met at. Head to the fountain on the south side of the park. A friend of mine will be conducting our business transaction on my behalf."

"No way. I don't do any business with anyone I've never met. Thanks for wasting my time."

"Preston, my friend, don't be so hasty."

"I was told you have the best product on the market. I'm willing to pay for it. But I'm not trusting my life to some random person. Especially if that person could be a cop."

"I'm sure I can persuade Cruz to meet you there."

I was quiet as though giving it some thought. "Fine. I'll see Cruz tomorrow at nine."

After disconnecting the call, I met my brother's gaze. "Looks like we're in business."

CHAPTER 17

I_T WAS_ times like these that the loneliness felt overwhelming. I stared around my empty living room. There weren't any family photos. No picture of a girlfriend's trip to the beach. In fact, my whole house seemed almost sterile. The closest friend I had was the giant fur ball sitting in my lap. *Had it always been this quiet in here?*

The quiet had never bothered me before. Until now. Now that Preston had been inside my house. I'd been tempted to change my sheets this morning, but I couldn't do it. I didn't want to lose his scent quite yet. God, how pitiful I was turning out to be.

Seeing Brody yesterday had freaked me out. I'd see the disappointment in Preston's eyes, and still, I couldn't admit to something between us. Why was it so hard for me?

Last night, I'd felt that deep, soul-awakening connection to him. I'd been lying there listening to him breathe, feeling his heartbeat under my hand on his chest. *This was what I felt two years ago.* The ever present heavy heart I usually experienced was gone. The one thing that was also gone...the guilt.

And then I felt guilty that I'd stopped feeling guilty.

Fuck. Twenty-one years of therapy and I was still just as fucked up now as I was as that thirteen-year-old girl.

I wanted to be courageous. Not just for him, but for myself. And the only one who could change was me. Taking one last look around my living room, I made a decision. "Wish me luck, Sherbie."

I set him aside, grabbed my coat, and ran out the door. Snow had settled on the ground. And it was still beautiful. Magical. I practically ran the few blocks to the el. I hopped on the train, this weird buzzing sensation in my belly the closer I got. Finally, I arrived. My knuckles connected with the door, and then I opened it. Our eyes locked, and I closed us inside the office together.

"Hi."

I didn't move further into the room, unsure of my welcome.

"What do you want, Landon?" Preston asked warily.

His defeated tone and posture hurt my heart. I'd done that to him. Had he given up on us, on me, already? I wouldn't blame him if he had.

"I fucked up yesterday when Brody showed up." I inhaled shakily. "I'm sorry. I hurt you, and that was the last thing I wanted to do."

He remained unmoved, but I kept going.

"I should have said...something. Instead, I did what I always do. And I'm sorry." I breathed a sigh of relief that I got it out. I hoped it was enough.

Slowly, Preston rose and strode toward me. My eyes drank him in from his broad shoulders to his tapered waist. His ink stood out against his skin, and I pictured all of the other tattoos and marking across his entire body. My fingers itched to touch all of them again. He stopped less than an arm's length away, and I had to tilt my head up to look into his eyes.

"I know you're trying. Yes, it hurt that after everything that was said between us, the minute my brother showed up, it was like none of it happened. But I can deal with that. I think having someone fight for you is something you're not used to, and it's freaking you out. That's okay. You'll get used to it. Because, Landon, I'm here to fight for you. You're worth it."

Throughout his entire speech, my heart raced, and now it nearly burst out of chest. I swallowed hard, trying to form words.

"Come with me. I want to show you something."

My forehead crinkled at the change of topic. "Um, okay."

Preston grabbed his coat off the rack near the door and ushered me down the hall and into the elevator. We stepped outside, and I shivered.

"My car's right over here."

He opened the door for me and then closed it once I was settled. Where was he taking me? My curiosity was killing me. I took in the neighborhood. This had been such a great area during my childhood. My mom had considered buying a house near here. Now, buildings were boarded up, graffiti was splattered over walls, and drug activity was on the rise. It was such a shame. It wasn't long before we pulled into a parking garage and parked in a spot on the first level.

Once again, Preston opened the door for me. Did other men still do this or was he just special? I couldn't contain my curiosity any longer as we walked down the sidewalk.

"Where are we going?"

Our hands accidentally brushed against each other's

while we walked and it sent a spark racing up my arm. It was a long-ingrained habit to widen the distance between us, but I stopped myself. There was this newly awakened part of me that wanted to twine our fingers together.

"You'll see."

I narrowed my eyes at his cagey response, but he just smiled and winked at me. We walked several more blocks before we stopped at a door. I spotted the sign in front. *Randolph Street Youth Recreation Center.* I glanced at Preston who opened the door for me.

It took several seconds for my eyes to adjust to the darkness inside the youth center after the bright sunshine of outside. The smell of sweat permeated the air and the sound of boisterous chaos and shoes squeaking and skidding across the wooden floor echoed around the entryway.

"Hey, Mr. Preston," a tall, gangly teenage boy greeted us, tripping over his feet as he came to a stop.

"How you doing, Lucas? How's that math class coming?"

He was all smiles. "I got my grade up to a C. The tutor is actually explaining things in a way I can understand."

Preston fist bumped him. "That's great, kid. Keep up the good work."

"I will. So, who's your pretty lady friend?"

A slight flush crept across my cheeks at the young boy's stare.

"This is my friend, Landon. Be nice to her. She's a little shy."

I sent him a narrow-eyed look before turning back with a wide smile and extended my hand. "Hi, Lucas. It's nice to meet you."

"You guys wanna come watch practice?" He bounced excitedly.

"Of course." Lucas took off and Preston laid his hand on my lower back, guiding me forward. *Practice?* I glanced around, curious what we were doing here. The humidity grew the closer we got to our destination. The thick air was enough to take my breath away. Close quarters and lots of sweaty kids was my guess. Lucas opened the door and the raucous shouts boomed loudly out into the foyer where we stood. In progress was a basketball game.

"Come on, let's go have a seat on the bleachers. The scrimmage should be over soon."

After we'd taken our seats I turned to him. "What are we doing here?"

"This is where I volunteer. I wanted to introduce you to a couple friends of mine."

My eyes widened.

"What?" Preston asked in response. "You don't think I'd be a good mentor?"

I shook my head. "No, it's not that. It's just a surprise."

Although, it shouldn't be. Not after hearing his story. It actually made so much sense. He'd been alone after Brody went off to college and he ended up making poor choices that affected his future. Trying to help other kids not make the same choices he had was something I could absolutely see Preston doing.

I looked out at the kids playing and back at him. "What exactly is it you do?"

"It's a little like a big brother program. I help them with their homework, or at least I try. I was never that great in school." His laugh was a little self-deprecating. "I'll take a couple of them out to the movies once in a while. I'm someone they can come to if they just need someone to talk to. Mostly, I try to keep them off the streets and out of trouble."

He was staring out at all the kids on the court, and I could see the pride in his eyes. I loved seeing this side of him. He was relaxed and in his element.

"What made you decide to become a mentor?"

His eyes took on this far away look. "Right before Brody and Ines left for Colorado, I got out of rehab. Again. For what felt like the millionth time. I left Pleasant Village, moved into a halfway house, and got a job with a construction company until I could get back on my feet. One day I was on my lunch break, and I saw these two kids over on the basketball court. They looked a few years apart in age, so I thought it was an older and younger brother taking a break from playing some one on one. Until I realized what was happening."

He paused, and I prompted him. "What happened?"

"It was a drug deal. The smaller kid, Jesus, he didn't look older than maybe twelve or thirteen. The older one was maybe nineteen or twenty. I took off running and they both scattered, but I caught up with the younger one." He actually smiled. "That kid, Lucas, man, he made me work to catch him."

My mouth dropped. "Are you telling me that the Lucas I just met and yours are one and the same?"

"Believe it."

"Oh my god. So, what happened?"

"He and I talked. Got to know each other. We discovered we were a lot alike. Single moms who worked several jobs. He has an older sister, but she's special needs. He was selling drugs to help his mom earn money."

"Wh—What? You're telling me that Lucas, at twelve or thirteen, was the one dealing? That makes me both sad and furious. What did you do?"

"I gave him a job."

A job? "Doing what?"

He shrugged. "I paid him to run errands for me. Pick up my mail at the post office. Get a few groceries here and there. Anything I could think of that could help him earn some money. He wasn't making nearly as much as he was dealing, but after we talked and I told him about my addiction, he decided it wasn't worth the risk. He's a smart kid."

I didn't have words. It was so much to take in.

"One day he asked if I would take him to a Cubs game. While we were there, it got me thinking. After I took him home, I made some calls, and, one thing led to another. Before I knew it, I was suddenly signed up to be a mentor here."

"That's incredible. When you first told me, I said I was surprised, but you know, I'm really not. You have such a huge heart. None of this surprises me at all. The only thing it does is make me more in awe of you." I looked away. "And a little unworthy, if I'm being honest."

He lightly gripped my chin and turned my head back to face him. "Don't you ever, not even for a fucking second, think that you're not worthy of anything and everything. Because you are. And me? It's just one more way for me to try and make up for all my sins. Of which there are so many."

Preston released me and we both went back to quietly watching the game. "Becoming a mentor for a bunch of teenagers was not ever something I saw myself doing. But I enjoy it. Some of them remind me of myself. I'd been so full of shit back then. Thought I knew it all. That I could conquer the world. Instead, the world fought back and kicked my ass."

"These kids are really lucky to have someone like you in their corner."

"I'm the lucky one." He stared out over the court, watching the kids play. "There are days that the cravings creep up on me out of nowhere. I'll come down here and hang out with the kids to remind myself that what I do is important. How can I be a role model for them if I'm pushing shit in my veins? I want to do things in my life that would have made my mother proud."

I clutched his hand tightly in mine. "I have no doubt she is."

Soon, the scrimmage wound down and several of the kids came over to say hi to Preston. It was clear they all adored him.

"Come on, I'll take you home. We need to talk anyway."

We headed outside and back toward the car.

"That sounds ominous," I said with a shaky laugh.

"Not really. I got a call from Felipe yesterday morning while I was with Brody. The deal is set up for nine tonight. We're meeting at the children's park on Berkshire, south side, near the fountain. The good thing about the location is that it's easily accessible from the street."

I tried picturing the area in my head, but details of the park were fuzzy, which I didn't care for. This whole thing made me nervous. It was too cold for us to get there early and wait, which I'm sure was purposeful. But it made me feel better knowing that it also decreased the chances of any of the bad guys lying in wait too long either.

"Hey. This isn't a first drug deal for either of us. We've

both been to plenty. You know how they work and things to watch for. It's going to be fine."

I just wished we had more time to prepare. But I had to trust him to know what he was doing.

We pulled in front of my house. I turned to Preston. "Thank you for taking me to meet your friends today. I enjoyed meeting them."

He smiled. "I'm glad."

Before I could stop myself, I leaned across the console, curled my hand behind his neck, and pressed my lips to his. I slicked my tongue against the seam, and he opened, pulling me inside. Every word I couldn't say, every emotion I was afraid to feel, I put into that kiss. Out of breath, I pulled back. "Please be safe tonight. I don't want to lose you."

Without waiting for a reply, I quickly jumped out of the car and raced into the safety of the house. My heart nearly thumped out of my chest. Every moment I spent with Preston made me forget why I shouldn't.

CHAPTER 18

"Are you sure you're ready?"

I glared at my brother. "You've asked me that ten times now. I don't understand why you guys are so worried."

"I don't understand why you're being so nonchalant. I get it. You've been doing this kind of thing for years. But you're not infallible, Preston. No matter how much you think you are." He ran his hands through his hair with a frustrated sigh. "You're not alone anymore. There are people who care about you. When people care, they worry."

Brody was right. I wasn't intentionally being blasé about things. It was just how I coped. Things could go wrong. I was meeting Cruz, who was not a fan. The thing that most worried me was that, for the first time in over a year, I would be in possession of the very thing I'd spent nearly half my life craving. The very thing that was almost always calling to me. The very thing that I'd let have far too much power over me.

"I know you all are worried, and I'm sorry you seem to think that I'm not. It's just easier if I don't think about anything but making the exchange and going on my way. Worrying makes a person nervous. And nervous people make mistakes." I shrugged into my coat and pulled my beanie over my head. "I'll see you when this is over."

"Be careful."

I gave a quick nod of acknowledgement before exiting the car. The night air burned my lungs. I jogged down the sidewalk, my shoes leaving footprints behind me in the newly fallen snow. I had a couple hundred burning a hole in my pocket. I checked both directions before dashing across the street. Not that there was much traffic in this neighborhood at this time of night.

It was nearly pitch black out here, with no streetlights on this side of the park. Any light that might filter through was cloaked by the cover of the tall pine trees that lined the perimeter of the street corner. The fountain was in a perfectly secluded location that, given better circumstance, might actually be a romantic spot for a picnic.

An image of sitting on a blanket in the summer shade with Landon popped into my head. I pushed it away. I needed to focus on what I was doing. The fountain slowly came into view, and the entire area surrounding it was deserted. It didn't surprise me. No doubt Cruz was close, and he was making sure I came alone.

I stood there in the freezing cold with my hands shoved in my pockets and my collar tugged up as high as it would go and waited. I didn't expect him to make me wait long. Just long enough to make me uncomfortable. I didn't look around to see if I could spot Landon or the Rodriguez men. Instead, I merely bounced on my toes trying to stay warm.

"Freezing my nutsack off out here," I mumbled to no one.

I couldn't know the exact time, but it seemed like an eternity had passed. Still, no one showed. *Was this some sort of test?* This whole cloak and dagger shit was getting old. If this was what it took to get confirmation, then I was on the verge of saying fuck it. I was going to assume Felipe was our guy and start surveillance on him anyway.

"I see you're still here," a voice called out just before Cruz stepped into view.

"You're lucky I am. It's fucking freezing out here. I was about ready to leave and let you explain to your boss why you're a couple of Benjamins short."

He sent me a look of pure hatred. "I don't like you."

I snorted. "Who the fuck cares?"

"More importantly," Cruz continued with a sneer, ignoring me completely. "I don't trust you. You stink of the cops. Their stench is all over you."

"Do you have my shit or not? I'm cold, and I'm ready to get the fuck out of here. I don't have time for your paranoia."

"Hold your arms out to your sides and spread your legs."

"Is this the part where you feel me up?" I smirked at Cruz.

"Shut your fucking mouth and do what I said, or we're going to have a problem."

I barely managed to stop my eye roll. Felipe sure knew how to pick 'em. My feet separated, and I raised my arms out. He patted nearly every inch of me down.

"Are you satisfied? Because I'm pretty sure you missed my junk."

"Let's just get this over with."

"Fine by me." I reached into my back pocket and pulled out the bills. Held between my first two fingers, I flipped them out toward Cruz. He snatched them out of my hand. Then, he reached into his pocket and pulled out a medium sized bag that even in the waning moonlight I could tell was filled with white powder. I couldn't spot the familiar purple wing shaped marking on it though. I held my palm out and just before he reached my fingertips, he dropped it on the ground.

"Oops."

Dick. I bent down and picked it up, my ears perked up for any sound of movement, but Cruz remained where he was.

"Pleasure doing business with you." I'd gotten what I'd come for.

Now it was time to get out of here and meet up with the team. I hadn't taken two steps before Cruz's voice stopped me. "I'm going to find out your secrets. And when I do, I'm going to kill you."

I didn't acknowledge his threat, although every nerve ending was on full alert. I didn't relax my guard until I'd escaped the confines of the park and was within sight of Brody and the car. Even then, I was listening intently for the sound of any other footsteps. Darkness lurked around every corner.

I collapsed into the passenger seat, my eyes staring straight ahead. "Drive."

"Did everything—"

"Drive," I barked.

The car turned over and we pulled away from the curb. Despite the hot air blowing out of the vents, my fingers trembled. Brody pulled out his phone and was speaking, but I couldn't hear anything beyond the buzzing in my ear. The scenery was nothing but a blur. I didn't see any of it. I don't know how long we drove, but suddenly, we were back at the office. I climbed out of the car with my brother silently following behind. We rode the elevator together, and he unlocked our office door, flipping on the light before settling into his chair. I dropped into mine and propped my head against raised fists taking deep breaths.

Cruz's threat lingered, and the baggie was burning a hole in my pocket.

"Landon and the guys are going to be here in a minute."

I nodded. Then, I could hear footsteps coming down the hallway. I raised my head, sucked in a final cleansing breath and blew it all out. By the time Landon burst through the door, I'd somehow managed to calm my racing heart and swallow back the nausea that threatened to rise.

"Are you okay?" She rushed over. I stood and she threw her arms around me, not caring about anyone else in the room.

I smiled, making it as genuine as possible. "Of course I am. I told you there was nothing to worry about."

I reached into my coat pocket, thankful my hands no longer shook and pulled out the baggie. There, stamped in bright purple ink was a set of angel wings.

CHAPTER 19

"HERE YOU GO. Now we know that Felipe is the one dealing *Rapture*."

Preston handed me the bag of coke. The way he rubbed his hand down his pant leg made me think he didn't want to be holding onto that baggie any longer than he had to.

"So, what's next?" I asked.

Preston nodded in Brody's direction. "Like I told my brother, now that we have confirmation Felipe is our guy, we're going to start surveillance. We'll follow him and Cruz from the club. See where they're going. Who they're talking to. See if we can get either of them to lead us to the bigger fish in the pond."

"How do you know he's not the biggest fish, already?"

"Felipe?" He laughed. "Not a chance."

"I'm going to let Brickman and Crawford know we found our guy. I'll send this to our techs and see if they can get a print or maybe some DNA off it. Find out who either of these guys are."

Preston nodded. "Sounds good. I wanted to mention

something. I could be wrong, it was pretty dark in both places, but there's a possibility that Cruz and Felipe are related somehow."

I paused. "What makes you think that?"

"I don't know. There was a slight resemblance. There was also a small something in their mannerisms. The way they held themselves. They seem similar. Who knows? I could be way off base."

"Hmmm, that might explain some things. Alright, well if you guys find anything, let me know."

I needed to get this stuff to my boss in the morning. He'd been harassing me over the last few days, badgering me about the progress of the investigation. I'd told Brickman and Crawford what was going on and they'd been checking on Elliott King. As of our last conversation, they hadn't been able to discover anything on him. Was it possible he wasn't involved in any of this? My instinct said he was involved, but if he was, he was a lot smarter than I was giving him credit for.

Suddenly, I didn't care about any of it. Not tonight anyway. I just wanted to be alone with Preston for a little while. Would these people ever leave?

As if reading my thoughts, Brody spoke up. "Everyone's tired. Let's all go home. Victor. Pablo. Thank you guys for being there tonight. We really appreciate it."

They all shoulder bumped each other and left. Brody straggled behind. He opened his mouth a couple time like he wanted to say something, but finally he shut it and then he too walked out the door, closing it behind him without a word.

It was just Preston and I, staring each other.

He broke the silence. "Thank you."

I hadn't expected that. "For what?"

"For trusting me." His voice was soft and uncertain.

"You're welcome."

I didn't want to admit that I'd never felt such fear as I had waiting for him to emerge from the trees. I'd seen him pause for several seconds after he'd picked up the bag off the ground and started walking away. His shoulders had jerked, and the movement had barely been there, but I'd seen it.

"What happened out there?" I sat down in the chair opposite Preston's desk.

His eyes met mine, but then darted away. "What do you mean? I met Cruz, we made the exchange, and then we came back here."

I studied him. "You paused too long before moving again for something not have happened. Did Cruz say something to you?"

Preston wouldn't look me in the eyes, and that scared me. He never hesitated. "Preston?"

He inhaled a shaky breath. "He suspects I'm a cop. Told me he'd figure out my secrets, and when he did," he paused. "He was going to kill me."

I swallowed the pebbles in my throat. "I see. Well, we're just going to have to make sure that doesn't happen. Won't we?"

"You know, I never really feared death. Not really. I mean, I'm honestly surprised I'm still alive actually. But, in that moment, I was terrified." The words came out thready. "For so long, I didn't think anyone would care if I died. I think, in the end, Brody would have been relieved. He would have grieved, of course, he's my brother. But after it was all said and done, a burden would have been lifted from his shoulders."

I clutched my trembling hands in my lap. Tears threatened to spill, but I was desperately trying to remain strong. For him. Because both of us couldn't break, and I suspected Preston was on the edge.

"But the moment he threatened me, the only thing I could think of was that,"—he raised his head and his eyes met mine—"I didn't want to leave you."

I raised my trembling fingers to cover my lips. Even after our night together a few days ago, I'd still been holding all these feeling back. I kept telling myself I didn't deserve to move on with my life. I deserved the pain. The penance. Hadn't I been punished enough? Was Preston placed in my path because it was time for me to find some measure of happiness?

"I don't want you to leave me either," I choked out, my voice like gravel. Pressure was building behind my eyes. I blinked it away. "Let's just put tonight behind us. Forget what happened, and deal with it tomorrow. Things will look different in the light of day."

He nodded, but his eyes still held that haunted glare. I rose from my seat and circled around to him. Preston swiveled in his chair and wrapped his arms around my waist pulling me to him. He rested his cheek against my stomach, and I threaded my fingers through his hair, holding him to me trying to lend him whatever strength I could. I don't know how long we stood like that, but it didn't matter. He took in a shaky breath. His hands began to roam, and he pulled away. He tilted his head back and stared up at me. Our gazes remained solely on each other even as Preston unbuttoned my jeans and slowly slid the zipper down. My breath hitched as he tugged them open and leaned forward to press a kiss to my lower belly. He peppered my skin with kiss after kiss, exposing more of my bare skin with each one until the next brush of his lips against me ghosted across the top of my sex.

"I want you," he whispered against me.

Preston didn't wait for a response. He merely yanked my jeans and underwear down to my ankles and then in one fluid movement picked me up and laid me across the top of his desk. I pulled my knees toward my chest, and he jerked my shoes and my bottoms completely off. He separated my knees, and before I could catch my breath, he buried his face in my pussy, his tongue and lips working together. He licked and nibbled his way to my clit, sucking it into his mouth and gently biting on it, sending a full body tremor through me.

"Yes," I moaned arching up and pressing myself against his face. His fingers tightened their grip on my hips, digging so deep into my skin he'd probably leave a mark.

My fingers tangled in his hair once again, clutching him tightly to me wanting, needing, more.

"Please," I begged.

"What do you want?" Preston whispered against my core, his breath making my skin even hotter.

"I need you inside me."

"Like this?" He slid a finger in, and I pulled him in deeper, but it wasn't enough. I shook my head.

"No. More."

"What about this?" Another finger slid in with the first and Preston pumped them in and out of me, keeping me right on the edge with his tongue nipping at my clit. His movements grew faster and harder. I chased the climax that was building until his teeth clamped down on my clit, and I screamed his name as it burst through me. My whole body tightened and then shook with tremors until slowly I came down. It wasn't enough. My pussy contracted against Preston's fingers still buried in me, but I wanted his cock.

"Not enough."

He withdrew, and I felt the emptiness. Preston quickly wrestled with his own pants and then there was the sound of foil ripping. He lined up with my entrance and pressed himself in. I pulled my knees back further into my chest, and he surged inside, his forearms caging my head. My fingers dug into his ass trying to pull him in deeper. Preston slammed hard against me at the same time his lips clashed against mine. The thrust of his tongue matched the pace of his cock as he pounded inside me. Faster and faster until I couldn't catch my breath.

We both needed to feel alive, Preston especially. I whispered words in his ear, but I wasn't sure what I was saying. It didn't matter. The only thing that mattered was we were together and in each other's arms. The world outside didn't exist. It was only Preston and Landon.

He kept up a punishing pace, and I met him thrust for thrust, encouraging him to go faster. Deeper. I wanted him to give me all he had and more.

"Fuck me. Make me yours," I spoke in his ear, biting down on it. He reached between us and furiously rubbed my clit hitting each nerve ending perfectly until my back arched and for the second time screamed out my release. It triggered Preston's and he slammed home a final time, his neck muscles stretched taut as he roared out his climax. Spasms shuddered through my body, as he collapsed against me, our breathing harsh. We remained connected until a shiver danced across my skin despite his body heat.

He brushed a kiss across my lips and then pulled out. I lowered myself off the desk with his help, stumbling a step.

While he disposed of the condom, I quietly pulled my underwear and jeans back on, and he did the same. Preston pulled me into his arms, and we held each other tight.

"I can't lose you," he whispered against my hair.

"You won't." I heard the promise in my words. Did he?

CHAPTER 20

I'D SPENT the first part of this morning working on a couple of the cases we had, but I was having trouble focusing. All I could do was replay the other night over and over again. And the fact I hadn't seen Landon since. After she and I had finished dressing, she'd taken me home. I'd almost called Brody, but it had been late, and I hadn't wanted to disturb him and Ines. With the baby coming in a few months, they needed all the sleep they could get. Besides, since we'd started our surveillance on Felipe and Cruz two nights ago, I didn't except to be getting much sleep in the near future either.

I glanced over at my brother. "What are you doing over there? You've been on your damn phone all day."

His cheeks took on a ruddy hue. "Just texting Ines."

Fuck. He probably meant sexting. Ines was a knock out, but I still shuddered. That was not information I needed to know.

"I need to get out of here for a bit. I'm going to walk over to Stan's and grab a couple sandwiches. What do you want?"

"Get me a pastrami on rye, will ya, please?"

"Sure. I'll be back in a bit."

Covered in my black leather jacket, I headed the few blocks over to the small, hole-in-the-wall diner I'd discovered the day we'd looked at the office space. Calling it a diner was pretty generous. In reality, it was more like a grocery store meat department without the rest of the grocery store. And they only sold cold cuts. There was a single two-seat table, but that was the only dining-in option.

The door opened and the bell chimed. A white-haired man with a matching white Sam Elliot mustache wearing an apron glanced up at my arrival.

"Afternoon. What can I get for you?"

"Can I get a pastrami on rye with provolone cheese and a reuben?"

"Coming right up."

I parked myself against the wall and waited. The door opened just as Stan finished the first sandwich. A young kid, late teens I'd guess, stepped just inside, rubbing his red, and most likely freezing, hands together. I took in his appearance. The large gray hooded sweatshirt almost swallowed him whole. He sniffed a few times and wiped his nose with his shirt sleeve. It was his eyes though... Even from ten feet away I could see his pupils were huge. There was something about the way he twitched and jerked that was familiar. I was also sure I'd seen him before.

"Hey, don't you play basketball over at the youth center on Randolph Street?"

His gaze darted over to meet mine, and I sensed his hesitation.

"I'm Preston. One of the mentors. My buddy Lucas hangs out over there. I thought I recognized you."

He produced a shaky smile. "Oh, yeah, I know Lucas. I think I've seen you around."

"You want a sandwich?"

"N—No, thanks. I'm good." He spun and darted out the door without another word.

I glanced at the man behind the counter whose worried gaze was still focused on where the kid had been standing. "What the hell was that about?"

"I'm not sure, but I can take a guess. I've been having some trouble lately."

"What kind of trouble?"

"A couple break-ins. Stole the small amount of money I keep in the cash register. Then last week a kid walked in off the street and robbed me at gun point. This neighborhood gets more dangerous every day. So many drugs coming through here. It's just not safe anymore."

Son of a bitch. There was no doubt that kid had been high as fuck. I just wasn't sure if, or what, he'd been planning when he'd walked through that door.

"Do you have any type of surveillance equipment?"

He shook his head. "Can't afford it. I'm losing more and more business each day. Too many people afraid to walk around the streets. This area is mostly old folks. It's why the drug dealers and criminals have started moving this way. There's no one to stand up to them."

I hated how defeated he sounded. There wasn't much I could do either. Not unless I could help get rid of some of the drugs. Maybe clean up the neighborhood a little. My body jerked. Was this what Brody had felt all those years? This incredible urge to do something good? To make a difference? Jesus, no wonder he'd started working for the D.E.A.

With sandwiches in hand, I made the trek back to the office, that kid's face staying with me the whole time. What the hell was I going to do?

～

"We're close to finding them, Michele, I promise. I'll talk to you soon." Brody disconnected the call with a sigh.

I barely noticed. For the last few hours, my mind had been elsewhere. I kept thinking about the kid from earlier today.

"What's going on with you? You've been acting weird ever since you got back from lunch."

"There was this kid that came into the diner while I was there. High as all get out. I don't know his name, but I'm sure I've seen him the youth center. I talked to him for a minute, and then he bolted. Almost like he'd panicked." Once again, I pictured the expression on his face. "Stan said there's been an increase in crimes, including against his shop. He's worried."

Brody sat upright. "Why didn't you tell me?"

I shrugged. "There wasn't anything *to* tell you. The kid walked in, we spoke for a minute, and he turned around and walked out. That was it."

"You just said he was on something. What if he'd wanted your money?"

"Then I would have given it to him."

I'd been that kid. High, wanting money, and after I'd tried taking it, our mother was dead. The scars on my arms burned.

"Not a day goes by that I don't think of her. Of what I did."

His shoulders deflated. "Guilt has a way of digging its claws so far into our soul, it's a wonder we can ever escape its clutches. I think you've been punished enough for what happened."

I didn't have any reply. It had been nearly twelve years, and there were nights my mother still visited me in my dreams. She never spoke. There was no anger, but neither was there forgiveness. Maybe it was her way of telling me my punishment would never be over.

I sighed in frustration. "I'll look for him at the rec center, and if I see him, I'll try and talk to him. Other than that, there really isn't much more I can do."

Doubts continued to creep in that I could do this. Was I really cut out for this kind of life? The one where I potentially "saved" people instead of being the one that needed to be saved. Fuck.

"Hey," Brody called out softly. "I don't know what's going on in that head of yours, but whatever it is, you can talk to me. I know it hasn't always been the case, but you're my brother, and I'm here for you. We're in a good place, and I don't want to lose that."

His words settled over me, bringing with them a tiny bit of peace. "We won't lose it. I just need to get used to having my brother again. I'll get there. Just give me a little time."

We stared at each other for several beats before he relaxed back into his chair, leaning back slightly. A loud crack sounded, and then Brody was tumbling backwards, arms flailing until he hit the floor. I stared in shock until I couldn't hold back my laughter any longer.

"Mother fucker." He scrambled to his feet and kicked the offending piece of furniture. "Piece of shit."

I barely got the words out. "I bet you're wishing now that you'd let me call my guy for office furniture, aren't ya?"

A sense of relief flowed through me. Everything was going to be all right.

CHAPTER 21

I WAVED AWAY the approaching hostess and strode through the nearly empty Monteverde toward the square four-top table near the back and its three occupants. What was a millionaire like Mr. King, with his designer suit, doing with two guys who were dressed like they shopped at a consignment store? I eased my pace as I spotted the gun the crewcut was carrying and pasted a pleasant smile on my face.

"Good afternoon, Mr. King."

The two men on either side of King stiffened at my arrival, but the businessman merely leaned back in his chair and threaded his fingers in his lap. His leering gaze traveled the length of my body, and a nausea-inducing grin crossed his features.

"Well, hello there, young lady. What can I do for you?"

"I'm Agent Roberts with the Drug Enforcement Administration. I was hoping you'd be able to answer some questions for me regarding a narcotic called *Rapture*."

He smothered the grin while the other two shifted in

their seats. I maintained a ready alertness in case either moved in a way I wasn't comfortable with.

"I'm not sure why you'd be asking me about that." King's lips pursed like he'd sucked on a lemon.

"We have reports that the drug is moving through your establishment, *Club Delight*. We'd like to track down its source. I was hoping maybe you'd heard some of your employees talking? Or maybe they'd heard or seen something. Any information you can share would be helpful."

He rose from his seat and slowly buttoned his suit jacket. As though that was some kind of sign, the other two men stood as well, their beady eyes scanning my body. All three towered over me. A heavy weight settled in my gut, but I straightened my shoulders and stared confidently back.

King took several steps until he stood directly in front of me. "I'm not sure what you're insinuating by coming here, Agent Roberts, but I'm a very wealthy and powerful man. Bad things have happened to people who have tried to interfere with my business. I recommend you watch yourself."

"Is that a threat, Mr. King?"

He merely grinned down at me. "Have a pleasant day."

King moved away from me and headed toward the front door. The silent men followed, both staring down at me as they walked past, the second one brushing against me, sending a cold chill down my spine. I stood there long after they'd gone, a sense of unease coursing through me. Finally forcing my body to move, I headed back to the office to talk to my boss.

~

Gibson had been pissed once I got back to the office and told him what had gone down at the restaurant. He'd stormed and raged about me going in there without any backup. I didn't remind him that he'd tasked Crawford and Brickman with following up some leads on the Sinaloa Cartel, which was another priority to Gibson.

I wanted to forget about the entire day. At least for tonight. Tomorrow would be soon enough to worry about things. Which was why I was standing in front of the door of apartment 2B. I missed Preston. Between their other cases, and the surveillance work he and Brody were doing on Felipe and Cruz, we hadn't had time to really talk.

Our relationship had changed the other night. It was heading in a direction I most definitely wasn't ready for. But I promised myself that I was going to give this thing between us a chance to become whatever it was going to be. A large part of me still didn't believe I deserved it, but I tried to push it away. Avoidance was something Dr. Carpenter and I talked about frequently. I'd become a pro at it. In this case, I think she'd approve.

I hadn't called beforehand. Maybe because I was hoping the man inside wouldn't be at home. *Stop avoiding, Landon.* I knocked on the door. Faint footsteps inside grew louder until they stopped, and I heard the lock on the other side disengage. A surprised Preston stood there looking at me.

"Hi," I smiled.

"Hey," he responded. That bourbon-smooth voice that never ceased to cause a shiver washed over me.

"Can I come in?"

Preston nervously gestured and stepped back. "Of course. What are you doing here?"

I entered his apartment, feeling a little self-conscious now that I was here. Still, I was going to do my best to stop hiding. "I missed you the last few days."

He relaxed at my words. "I missed you too."

There was an uncomfortable silence. Since I was trying not to push him away, I wasn't sure how to act. Usually Preston was the one doing the chasing. He was the confident one. The bold one. Now it seemed as though the both of us were treading uncharted territory.

He shook himself out of the quiet. "Do you want something to drink? I don't have much to choose from. Water or Dr. Pepper."

"No, thanks, I'm good. Huh, I didn't expect this to be so weird," I chuckled nervously.

"Oh, is it weird? I hadn't noticed," Preston deadpanned.

I couldn't resist sticking my tongue out. "Very funny. But I'm really glad I'm not the only one who thinks so."

He reached out and tugged my hand, pulling me toward the couch. "Come on weirdo. Have a seat. Then we can talk about why you're here. Besides missing me, I mean."

We sat on the couch together, with Preston pulling my legs and setting them over his lap. He started massaging my feet. I tried tugging them out of his grip, but he only tightened his hold.

"Just sit there and relax."

Knowing it was easier to let him have his way than to resist, I sat back against the arm of the couch so he could continue. It wasn't long before I let out a sigh of contentment. Soon, I started getting drowsy, and my eyes grew heavy. I was vaguely aware of my surroundings. I was jostled and my eyes fluttered. It felt like I was moving, but the warmth cocooning me made me close them again.

THE STRONG SCENT OF SPRING AND SUNSHINE FILLED MY NOSE. My gaze darted around until it landed on Preston. He was shirtless and propped up against his headboard reading through some files. The lamp on his bedside table was lit casting a soft glow around the room. I shifted and his eyes met mine. He smiled.

"Hello, again," he whispered.

"Hi. Why did you let me fall asleep?" my voice was scratchy. I raised an eyebrow. "And how did I conveniently end up in your bed?"

"For one, you looked like you needed the rest. Besides, you haven't been asleep long. Thirty minutes maybe. And for two, the last bed we were in was yours. I figured I'd share mine this time."

"I bet." I chuckled and tucked my hands under my chin. I stared up at him. "What are you working on?"

Preston flipped the papers. "I'm going over surveillance photos of Felipe and Cruz. There are a couple guys in a few of these pictures, but I don't know if they're our suppliers or not."

"If they are, we'll find them."

"I know we will." He glanced down at me with a sigh and closed the folder before setting it aside. "I've just never been long on patience."

"I don't know. You've been pretty patient with me."

He smiled a little smugly. "I have, haven't I?"

I huffed out a small laugh.

Preston's expression shifted and turned serious again. "Can I ask you a question?"

"Sure," I replied nervously.

"What were you doing at the hotel that night?"

I should have expected this. There didn't seem to be much that Preston hadn't shared with me about his life. It was only reasonable that with this step forward in our...relationship, that he wouldn't want to know things about me and mine. I just wasn't ready to give him all the answers he was looking for. Not yet. I could still give him part of the truth, if not all of it.

"It was the anniversary of my father's death."

He scooted down until he too lay on his side facing me. He reached out and brushed my hair back. "I'm sorry."

I shrugged. "It's been twenty-one years and it never gets any easier."

"You must have been young when it happened."

"Thirteen."

"That's a rough age to lose a parent. Were the two of you close?"

"Not really. He and my mother had divorced the year before. She'd had full custody, but he took her to court for partial custody. It was pretty ugly. In the end, he won, and I was to spend my summer breaks with him. My dad had a lot of...mental health issues."

"Still, it's hard losing a parent. I never knew my dad. He left right before I was born. Brody filled the void, so I never really missed him. But my mom. I miss her every single day. It only makes it worse knowing that I'm the reason she's not here."

It was eerie how similar our sins were.

"What made you decide to work for the D.E.A.?"

I blinked at the change in topic and relaxed muscles I'd tightened unconsciously. This was a much safer line of questioning. "My mom had remarried shortly before my dad's death, and when I was fifteen, my step-dad got a job offer in D.C. So, we left Chicago. After I graduated high school, I stayed in D.C. and ended up going to Georgetown University." I chuckled. "Can you believe I was actually thinking about becoming a lawyer?"

Preston's eyes widened. "You? A lawyer?"

"Yeah. I'd been considering some type of law enforcement, but I didn't want to necessarily be a police officer. I worked toward my degree in criminal justice. During one of my classes, I did a research paper on the Drug Enforcement Administration, and immediately, I was intrigued. As soon as I finished my paper, I knew exactly what I wanted to do." I shrugged. "I went on to get my Bachelor's, with a major in Criminal Justice and a minor in statistics. Then I got my Master's. Once I graduated, I applied to work for the D.E.A. Took me over a year to be accepted. I went through the training and graduated from Quantico at the top of my class."

"When did you meet my brother? He never told me. I knew you'd been his handler, but that was about it."

I covered my face with my hand. "I'd moved back to Chicago and was four, maybe five, months out of Quantico. Director Gibson told me he needed to see me. I was scared shitless. He's an intimidating bastard. I thought for sure I was being fired already. I walked into his office and there stood this dark and intensely brooding man."

Preston laughed. "Intensely brooding sounds exactly like Brody."

"Lord was he ever. Anyway, Gibson introduced us. Your brother had been assigned a handler already, but for a reason only the two of them knew, he asked for someone else."

"And you were that someone else." It wasn't a question.

"Apparently so. He explained in explicit detail what my job would be, and how his life was, essentially, in my hands. I almost pissed myself. I mean, that was a lot of responsibility for someone who hadn't even been on the job half a year."

"Everything obviously worked out, since you're both still here."

"I guess so."

"Do you enjoy what you do?"

I thought about the question. "I don't know that anyone really *enjoys* it. Day in and day out we see almost the worst of humanity. The drugs. The death. The continuous need for power and money, no matter who gets hurt in the process. It's a lot. I will admit to a rush of excitement each time we go out on a seizure. It feeds the adrenaline junkie in me. I also get a sense of satisfaction when the bad guys get what's coming to them. But in the full sense of enjoyment from my job, I'm not sure that I do."

"Well, Brody has nothing but respect for you. He doesn't trust a lot of people, but I know you're close to the top of the list."

"Your brother trusted me with his life without even knowing me. No way was I letting him down. I didn't want his death on my conscience."

He leaned over and ghosted a kiss across my lips. "I trust you with my life, as well."

"I hope I don't let you down."

Preston shook his head. "Not a chance."

His earlier question had me curious as well. "What about you? You never told me why you were at the hotel."

"I was part of the construction crew in charge of the hotel

renovations. It's one of the few jobs I'm actually qualified for that my sponsor can usually find for me every time I get out of rehab. I don't love it, but it's better than sitting on my ass staring at a computer all day. I needed something that kept me busy."

I nodded. "I completely understand. After your brother resigned from the organization, I decided to switch from being an agent on the streets to an intelligence analyst. I was good at my new position, but I didn't have the passion for it like I did being a field agent."

"Earlier that day, while I was on my break, I went into the bathroom. One of the guys from the crew was in there doing a line. He turned and offered me some."

I couldn't hold back my gasp.

"As you know, I never hide my scars, so it wasn't a big secret that I used. Or at least that I used to. Either way, I turned him down. He shrugged it off and went back to work as though nothing had happened. But the rest of the day, all I could think about was seeing him take that hit."

"Did you tell anyone what he'd done?"

Preston's expression said that was a dumb question. "I wasn't a narc. Besides, I needed that job, and it was my word against his. He'd been there longer and had a lot of friends. After work was over, I knew if I left that hotel, the first thing I'd do was track down my old dealer. I stayed there with the hopes that I could quiet the urge. That's when I saw you."

I stared at him. How different things would have been for both of us if Preston hadn't been there that night. I wasn't sure I believed in fate or destiny, but there had to be a reason why he was placed in my path. "And now? Do you still have the urges?"

It was a question I wasn't sure I wanted the answer to.

"I won't lie and say no. Sometimes, though not often, the urge is constant, picking at me like a scab. Nearly all the time, it's quietly simmering beneath the surface, but instead of a mighty roar, it's a soft whisper I can usually tune out. There's been the rare occasion when they completely disappear, if only temporarily."

"Like when?"

"Usually when I'm with you. That night, for instance. The minute I saw you, they crept away. I didn't notice until right before I was about to leave. Before you asked me to stay, I'd been sitting in that bar for hours, watching you, and not once did I think about using."

"You watched me for hours? And you called *me* a weirdo?" I poked him in the chest. It was a little disconcerting that I'd been oblivious enough to my surroundings that Preston had observed me for so long and I hadn't even noticed.

Even in the pale light, I saw his cheeks flush. "I admit it was slightly creeper behavior, but I couldn't help it. Something about you drew me in, and I couldn't stop. I didn't even think about leaving. All I wanted to do was find out what was bothering you, and make it go away."

I reached out and cupped his cheek. "That's exactly what you did. You made my pain go away. I felt a little guilty about putting that burden on you. It wasn't really fair of me." My eyes scanned his face. "I'm glad I did it, though. Otherwise, I don't think we'd be here. In this place. Together."

Preston pulled me tight against him and pressed a kiss to the top of my head. "I don't know. Something tells me we still would have met."

I cuddled closer, inhaling the scent that was all him. "I think you're probably right."

But would I still feel like I was falling in love?

CHAPTER 22

"Good morning."

I turned at the sound of Landon's sleepy voice. Even with bed head and covering her mouth with a yawn, she still made my heart skip a beat. "Morning. Kinda hoping you're not a coffee drinker, because I don't have any. I do have milk and cereal though."

She sent me a lazy smile. *God, I could wake up to her every day.* "I am a coffee drinker, but I'll grab a cup on my way to work. There's a coffee shop on the corner."

"I know. That might have been where I'd done a little stakeout waiting for you to get off work the day I followed you to the train station." I sent her an abashed smile.

Her eyes widened and she placed her hands on her hips. "Seriously, Preston? You really are quite the stalker, aren't you?"

I just shrugged. "What can I say? I get what I want any way I can."

Landon moved to stand next to me in the kitchen and

poured herself some cereal in the bowl I'd left her. She hip-bumped me. "Hand me that milk, you creeper."

We ate in companionable silence, and then she helped me wash the dishes. "What do you have planned for the day?"

"I've got some more reconnaissance to do. I think I found another lead, this one to our Mr. King. I also need to head over to the rec center. Lucas called me yesterday. He's having a bit of trouble and wanted to talk. Not sure what it's about yet. He was awfully cagey. What about you?"

Landon fidgeted. "I talked to King yesterday."

I straightened. "What? Where?"

She bit my lip nervously. "At Monteverde."

"What aren't you telling me?" I didn't like the way she avoided meeting my eyes.

"He was there with two guys that looked like muscle." She paused. "There might have been a veiled warning before he left about interfering with his business."

I slammed the dish towel on the counter. "Why the hell are you just now telling me this? You had all night."

"Because I didn't want you to worry. My boss already knows what happened."

A sickening sensation settled in my gut. "How could I not worry, Landon? Jesus."

She closed the distance between us and laid her hand on my chest. It didn't do anything to calm the rage inside me. "Nothing's going to happen to me. Believe it or not, I know what I'm doing. And I've already promised that if I do any more questioning, Brickman and Crawford will be with me. They'll make sure nothing happens to me."

It didn't do much to quell the worry, but there wasn't much I could do. This was part of Landon's job, whether I liked it or not. "Just be fucking careful."

She nodded. "I will. I promise. I need to get home so I can shower and change. I have a lead I want to pursue, as well. One of the agency's informants called in a couple days ago and said he found one of his buddies dead. Overdosed on *Rapture*. But he was able to give me a name. Eli. Ring any bells?"

I thought about all the names I'd gathered, but that one hadn't come up. "No. The only other name I've been able to come up with is Silas in a conversation Brody had overhead when he was tracking King. They'd been in a discussion… fuck, why didn't I think of this? Wait a minute."

I ran back into my room and grabbed the file I'd thrown on my nightstand last night. Shuffling through page after page and picture after picture, I came across one Brody had snapped outside King's delivery company two days ago.

"Were these the two guys with King yesterday?" I gave her the picture. "This is him and a couple of guys he's been seen with in multiple meetings. The one in the center with the longer dirty blond hair is Silas, although I have no idea who exactly he is. The man on the right, with the crewcut, is unknown."

Her eyes scanned the page. "Yes, that's them."

"Fuck. See if your informant tags him as this Eli guy. My guess is, it's him."

Landon nodded. "You're probably right. If, on the off chance, my contact doesn't know him, I'll run the picture through facial recognition and see if I can get a hit."

"Sounds good." I looked at the clock. "Shit, it's getting late. I need to get in the shower, too. Are you sure you don't want to jump in with me and save water?"

Despite the seriousness of only moments ago, Landon

burst out laughing and rolled her eyes. "Thanks for the offer, but I'll run home quick. Clean clothes and all, you know?"

"Hey, I'm just trying to do what I can to save the environment." I waggled my eyebrows at her.

"I'm sure Mother Nature thanks you for your effort. Speaking of, thank you for breakfast. You take your shower and check in with me later. Tell Lucas I said hello, will you?"

I tugged her against me, and she circled her arms around my neck.

"Should I be jealous that you want me to tell another man you said hello?" I growled.

Landon giggled. "He is quite the cutie. You never know. Lucas just might come right in and sweep me off my feet if you're not careful."

"Then I better do everything I can to make you choose me."

Her fingers brushed across my forehead and then down my cheek. "I don't think you have anything to worry about. No matter who it was, I'd choose you. Each and every time."

Our eyes locked, but no words passed between us. Because no matter how far we'd come, Landon wasn't quite ready to hear all the things that needed to be said between us. Not yet, anyway. Since those feelings couldn't be spoken in words, then they had to be expressed through touch. I lowered my lips to hers and put all my emotions and words into my kiss.

With every brush of my tongue against hers there was hope. Joy. Faith. But most of all, there was love. The kiss was soft and gentle. Taking my time, I drew out each and every touch, teasing and tantalizing making sure she felt what I was trying to say. There was almost a desperation in her response as though she wanted me to understand she felt it all too.

Breathless, we separated. I rested my forehead against hers. "I'd choose you too."

We stood there for another moment, and I soaked up this moment, because it seemed like a turning point. "Be careful and call me later."

She nodded. "I will."

I locked the door behind her and took a quick shower before heading down to the youth center. Lucas had me a little worried.

The door of the youth center squeaked. I made a mental note to talk to Director Hawkins about getting the spring oiled. The familiar scent of body odor, sweat, and floor polish permeated the air. Despite the aroma, this place was like a second home. I loved coming here. I loved the kids. Brody had been proud of the fact that I'd become a mentor.

It hadn't been a conscious effort to make him proud, but knowing that he was gave me a sense of accomplishment. As though I hadn't completely fucked up my life. It also got me thinking about my own future and whether or not I saw myself having kids. They were never really anything I'd thought of before. Not until recently. Not until Landon.

Lucas was usually in one of the study rooms, so I went in search of him. Three empty rooms later, and I still hadn't been able to find him. The only other place he might possibly be was the basketball court.

"Hey, Mr. Preston," a few of the kids greeted me as I passed, and I waved hello.

I tugged open the door to the gymnasium, but it too was empty. I heard a faint cry from the direction of the locker rooms. Just then the door burst open and Lucas came tumbling out with a yell. "Mr. Preston, come quick, it's Owen."

My shoes slapped across the shiny wood floor, and I skidded to a near stop to avoid colliding into him as he stood there with tears pouring down his face. I scooted past him, and he grabbed my arm, tugging me down the narrow passageway between lockers.

We turned a corner, and I spotted the body on the floor. "Fuck," I cursed and dug out my phone, tossing it to Lucas. "Call 9-1-1, now. Tell them we need an ambulance."

I didn't wait for him to follow my command. Rolling the body over, I cursed again. This was the same kid from Stan's Diner the other day. His lips were blue, and his face was ashen. On the floor next to him was a fucking baggie with those goddamn purple angel wings.

He wasn't breathing. "Come on, Owen."

I curled my hand over the other and immediately started driving them into his chest. The crunch of his ribs under my palms made me nauseous, but I didn't stop pushing.

Push.

Push.

Push.

Keeping a steady rhythm, sweat dripped off my forehead, but I didn't stop. I heard the buzzing of voices behind me, but I couldn't decipher what was being said.

"Breathe, Owen. You can do it. Please. Just breathe." *Goddamnit, Owen, breathe.*

I felt someone tugging on my arm, but I kept pressing down on his chest over and over.

"Sir."

"Sir."

The word penetrated my brain, and I looked up, my body still moving. A paramedic filled my vision. "Sir, let us take over."

Clumsily, I rose to my feet and took a few steps back, my hands hanging at my sides, giving the paramedics room to continue working on Owen. My chin dropped to my chest as I tried to catch my breath. One of the men glanced up at me. "You saved him."

You saved him.

You saved him.

A small hand clasped mine, and I looked down to see Lucas standing next to me. I slid my hand from his and wrapped my arm around his shoulder, tugging him into my side. We moved further away from the scene and sat on the nearest bench. He huddled even closer to me, softly crying and wiping his nose on his sleeve.

"It's alright. He's going to be okay." I said quietly. "What happened?"

He sniffed. "I was out in the gymnasium shooting some free throws waiting for you, and I had to go to the bathroom. Owen was already in here. I told him not to do it, but he wouldn't listen. It happened so fast. One second he was standing there, the next, he was on the floor. I didn't know what to do."

"You did the right thing, Lucas," I assured him. "Don't worry, he's going to be okay."

Within several minutes, the director, several firefighters, and two police officers spilled into the locker room. The paramedics loaded Owen onto a stretcher.

"Mr. Hawkins is going to call your mom. He'll stay with

you until she gets here. I'll talk to the police, but they may want to ask you a couple questions. Tell them exactly what you told me, okay?" I knelt down in front of Lucas and pulled him into a hug. "I'm going to find out who did this, and I promise I'll make them pay."

He swiped his palms across his tear-stained face, and I stood to meet Hawkins' eyes. "Take care of him."

"I will."

I pivoted and escaped the confines of the locker room, my rage growing with every step I took. No more surveillance. No more waiting and seeing. Whoever was behind this shit needed to be stopped. It was time to move this timetable up.

CHAPTER 23

I WEAVED my way around the homeless encampment, trying to ignore the bitter cold, while I searched for Bernie. He'd been an agency informant for the last couple years. He had his ear to the ground, and if anyone could get me some more intel on some of these guys, it would be him.

People huddled around metal barrels of fire trying to stay warm, while others had layers upon layers of blankets and other materials draped over their tents in order to keep the blistering cold wind from penetrating the thin fabric. More than once, local LEOs had attempted to make everyone disband. They'd end up relocated somewhere new before moving back here.

I stepped over piles of refuse and dodged nearly getting run over by a man chasing another. Finally, I spotted my contact standing near a fire, his hands hovering over the flames.

"Agents Roberts, good to see you."

"You too, Bernie. I hope you're staying warm."

He shrugged. "Doing the best I can. I found me a room

over at this gal's place. She lets me stay there once in a while."

"That's good. Take her up on it as often as you can, will ya?"

"Yes, ma'am. You know I will." He nodded. "Now, what can I do for you?"

"First off, I'm sorry about your friend."

He shrugged. "It's just one more death in a long string of them out here on the streets."

"Still, I'm sorry. I was hoping I could ask you a couple questions about it."

"Sure thing. I don't know if I have an answer, but I'll do my best."

I reached inside my coat and pulled out the picture Preston had handed me this morning. "Do you recognize any of these men?"

He took the pic from me and unfolded it. His eyes scanned each face, and I held my breath, hoping that this would give us the lead we needed. Bernie handed the picture back to me.

"I've seen a couple of them around."

"Is one of them this Eli you mentioned?"

He glanced around. Only a few stragglers were in our immediate area. He leaned in closer and lowered his voice. "Yeah, the crewcut is Eli. I think the other one's name is Silas. I don't know the fancy man in the suit."

He straightened and stared into the fire, rubbing his hands together and then hovering them over the flame again.

"Do you know what they might be involved in? I'm looking for those who are part of this new drug called *Rapture*."

"I can't say for a hundred percent, but I know there are a couple new dealers. Felipe is one of them."

I nodded. "Yes, we know about him already, but I'm trying to figure out where he's getting his supply. And who that person is working for."

"Sorry, Agent. I don't know much more than that."

It was disappointing, but at least I'd gotten confirmation on the man named Eli. It was something.

"No, thank you, Bernie. You've been extremely helpful."

"Anytime."

"Be careful out here and try to stay warm, alright?"

He smiled crookedly. "Yes, ma'am."

I made my way back to where I'd left my car parked. Halfway there, my phone rang. It was Preston.

"Hey. You okay?"

"No. Can you come to the office?"

I heard something uneasy in his voice. "Of course. Give me about thirty minutes."

He didn't even say goodbye. I rushed the rest of the way to my car, my boots clomping on the sidewalk. I slid on a patch of ice before I reached it, but recovered my balance before falling on my ass. I hadn't liked the short response from Preston. Something was wrong.

Trying to maintain the speed limit, I navigated the roads, changing lanes, and impatiently tapping my fingers on the dashboard at red light, before finally reaching the office.

By the time I got to their door, my chest was tight with anxiety. I didn't knock. Instead, I barged in, my eyes moving straight to Preston's desk. His gaze met mine and a fiery rage burned in his hazel depths. On top of his desk, he clenched and unclenched his fists. Brody, who'd been on the phone, disconnected the call.

"What's going on?" I glanced between the two of them.

"We've had a change of plan," Brody said. "We're waiting on Victor and Pablo to get here. They're on their way."

I moved to sit. "What's this change of plan?"

"We're scheduling another deal, and, this time, we're making an arrest," Preston bit out.

"What happened?"

"I went to the youth center to talk to Lucas. Found a fucking kid overdosing on this shit in the bathroom."

My hand went to my mouth. "Oh my god. Is he okay?"

"We think so," Brody interjected. "Paramedics took him to the hospital, but we haven't been able to get any confirmation on his status."

I collapsed back into my chair as though all the air had been let out of me. Jesus. "So, we arrest these guys, and then what? Try to get them to give us their supplier's name?"

Brody nodded. "That's the plan."

"What if they don't? Give up their supplier, I mean?"

"A kid almost fucking died today. There's a big difference between a drug charge and attempted murder."

"We don't have any proof that this kid bought the stuff from Felipe."

"Once Owen gets better, he is a key witness. He can lead us to who sold it to him. Plus, we know for a fact that Felipe and Cruz are involved. We only have to follow the trail."

Preston wasn't going to let this go. Not that I blamed him. His rage was evident. "So we set up the new deal like the last time?"

"Yes."

"Okay, I'm in."

He gave a single nod.

"How are you going to make contact? You don't have his number, do you?"

"I have the number he called me from. I'm going to try that."

"And if that doesn't work?"

"Then I'm going to *Club Delight*."

"If you do, I'm going with you," I told him.

Preston snapped out a denial. "No way."

I crossed my arms. "Yes. You're not in the right frame of mind to handle this rationally. You're too close. If you want to bring these guys down, we can't let anything derail this investigation. And, right now, you're not handling your rage."

"She's right," Brody interrupted. "Look at you. You're barely suppressing your anger. How are you going to keep your shit together once you're actually face to face with this asshole? Landon will be there to help keep you calm. You need her."

After a quick nod of thanks, I turned back to Preston. "We're in this together, remember? You and me."

I could see his jaw tightening and his lips pressing together. "Fine, but that's a last resort."

"You better hope that number works then. Are you going to be okay to place the call?"

"I will be by the time Victor and Pablo get here. I'm going to take a short walk."

Preston rose from his chair and I followed, but he held up a hand. "I need to be alone for a minute. Please."

I settled back in my chair, giving him the space he asked for. He walked out of the office leaving me alone with Brody.

"You and my brother seem to have figured things out."

"We're trying. Well, I am. I don't think Preston's ever had

any doubts about how things are supposed to be between us."

He laughed a little at that. "I think you're right about that. I was surprised, to say the least."

"I don't think anyone was more shocked than me to discover he was your brother."

"He's different now. With you, I mean. There's this new sense of maturity." He shook his head. "No, that's not really it. Maybe more grounded. Serious."

"I don't think you give your brother enough credit."

"Yeah, maybe you're right." Brody stared, studying me. "Does he know?"

I didn't have to ask what meant. "No."

His lips turned down. "Are you going to tell him?"

"Eventually. When I'm ready."

"You're both a lot alike, you know?"

"I know. He told me about your mom. I'm sorry. I can't imagine how hard that was...for both of you. I understand now why the two of you were always butting heads. I'm really glad you've been able to reconcile. Preston looks up to you."

"We've definitely come a long way over the last year. The things I did while undercover made me realize that we all make mistakes. It's how we respond to them that matters. He's worked harder than anyone I know to atone for his sins."

"I think he's finally learning to forgive himself."

Brody's expression shifted and was almost full of pity. "What about you? Have you learned to forgive *yourself*?"

I looked away from his penetrating gaze. Had I?

CHAPTER 24

THE NUMBER WORKED.

We'd set up another deal for tonight. Felipe said he would be there to personally handle it. Which made things a whole lot easier. The deal had been set for inside the park again. There were distinct disadvantages to that for us, but we'd decided to bring in Landon's co-workers Brickman and Crawford. That way we had all possible exits from the park covered.

"We need to set you up with a wire this time," Victor announced. "The recording will be used as part of the evidence. We need the verbal confirmation of who you're talking to and what they're selling."

It didn't set well with me, but he was right. Everything about this had to be by the books. We had to have proof. Which meant wearing a wire, no matter how much I was against it.

"Fine."

"Manuel is usually in charge of our AV needs, but he had to work tonight. So, you're stuck with me." Victor smiled good-naturedly. "The good news is, we got the hook up. Here, put these on."

He held out a pair of glasses. I turned them this way and that, but they looked like a normal pair of glasses. I slipped them on, and Pablo pulled out a small, black device that looked similar to a gaming remote control. He flipped a switch and static filled the office and a grainy picture displayed on the screen. It was Victor, who flipped me off.

"Holy shit, are these for real?" My voice echoed back at me from the device in Pablo's hand.

"Here, these are for everyone." In Victor's hand were tiny earbuds. "We'll be able to hear what's going on during the exchange while that device over there will record it."

I looked at Brody. "We need to get a pair of these."

He shook his head and stared around the room. "The last time this happened, they met in the darkened corner by the fountain. Our visibility is severely limited. Which means, regardless of your fancy glasses, we're going to have to be a lot closer. Let's go over the plan one more time."

ONCE AGAIN, BRODY AND I WERE SITTING IN HIS CAR. "YOU ready? As hard as it might be, you need to keep it together. Think about what this will mean for Owen. We want justice for him. For all the other people who have been killed by this shit. Being pissed is good. But make sure that you use your anger in a productive way."

Words clogged my throat, so I only nodded. *I can do this. I will do this.*

"Everyone's in place. As soon as you have the product, step out of the way. It should be smooth and easy."

I was twitchy with nervous energy and just wanted this to be over. I tugged the door handle, but Brody stayed me with his hand on my arm. I glanced over at him. "Be careful."

"I will."

Shutting the door behind me, I loped across the street and made my way to the familiar spot by the fountain. Felipe and Cruz were both there. As well as two other men I didn't recognize. *Why were they here?* I slowed the closer I got, coming to a stop in front of them.

"You're late."

"Traffic." I chin jerked in the direction of the two new guys. They were on full alert and scanning the area. One shifted, and it looked like he had a gun strapped to his side. The crew could see and hear what I was seeing, but just in case, it was probably a good idea to give them a heads up. None of us expected two more players in this game. "Who are they? Your bodyguards?"

Felipe glanced over his shoulder and then returned his gaze to me. A smirk tilted up one side of his lips. "They're my insurance policy."

"Your insurance policy? Against what? I'm here to make a simple exchange, and then I'll be on my way. I don't get why you insist on making deals outside. It's fucking freezing out here."

"You're a special case."

My nerves were stretched about as thin as they could get. There was a tone to his words that had me on edge. Like he was toying with me.

"Whatever, man. Do you have my shit or not? I'm ready to go."

Cruz and the other two men spread out, effectively caging me in.

"Yes, about that. We seem to have a problem."

"What problem is that? I have money. You have the drugs. Not seeing a problem here."

"Well, you see, Cruz here did a little bit of digging. Would you like to know what he discovered?"

I tried to continue playing it cool, but fuck if I didn't hope that the cavalry was closing in. Because something told me some bad shit was about to go down.

"I'm sure you're going to tell me." My gaze homed in on Felipe. I couldn't worry about the other three. I had to trust the gang to have my back.

"Seems you have a brother."

Fuck. I shrugged. "Yeah. I'm still not seeing the problem here."

His laughter sent a shiver of dread along the back of my neck.

"Brody Thomas used to be a D.E.A. agent. Now the two of you work together at your own private investigation firm."

I waved my palms toward him. "I think you have me confused with someone else."

In a flash, Felipe withdrew a gun from behind his back. I didn't think, I just moved. But it was too late. The sound of gunfire filled the air.

"Son of a bitch." I slapped my hand over my stinging side, and I could feel the warm wetness against it. There was no time to look and see how bad it was, because I scrambled behind the fountain. Dirt and concrete exploded around me, pieces of shrapnel pinging off my skin as I lay on my side with my hands covering my head.

"Preston!" Landon screamed.

"I'm fine," I hollered back.

The smell of blood and gunpowder soon permeated the air, and I was practically gagging on it. I couldn't see shit from where I was tucked behind the fountain, but the sound of bullets being exchanged slowly died down until a lone single shot echoed and then faded.

"Everyone check in." I recognized Brody's voice.

"Here."

"We're all good."

"I'm okay."

Slowly, I rolled sideways, and used the edge of the concrete bank to pull myself up. I looked around to find Cruz and the two bodyguards lying on the ground. Victor and the two D.E.A. agents were standing over top of them, but no one was moving. Pablo had Felipe face down, cuffing him and reading him his Miranda rights.

My eyes fell to Landon. She was staring back at me, her face white and tears in her eyes. Before I could blink, she ran to me and threw her arms around my neck. I winced in pain, but wrapped my free hand around her, pulling her close and nuzzling my nose in the crook of her neck, breathing in her lavender and vanilla scent.

"It's okay," I whispered in her ear.

"I thought I was going to lose you." Her words were muffled against my chest.

"Just a flesh wound." I was starting to feel the blood loss, though.

"Fuck, Preston." Brody skidded to a stop in front of us.

I glanced up at him. "I'm all right, I think."

"Let me take a look."

Landon reluctantly pulled back from me, and I tugged up my shirt with a hiss of pain. My brother examined the wound.

"It doesn't look too bad, but you might need stitches. We need to have a doctor check you out."

Normally, I'd protest, but based on Landon's expression, that wasn't going to be an option. Terror was written on her face. I didn't want to be the continued cause of that.

"Fine. Everyone else is okay, I take it?"

"Yeah, we're good." Victor called out. "We called this in. Although I'm sure the cops are already on their way. We'll wait for them. You guys go ahead to the hospital."

I nodded my thanks.

Landon spoke up. "I'll take him. Brody, why don't you go home. I'm sure Ines is worried."

My brother hesitated. I could tell from his expression he wanted to argue. He nodded. "Call me once you're all patched up."

"I will."

CHAPTER 25

Preston refused the emergency department, saying it would take far too long to see someone for a couple of stitches. Against my better judgement, I took him to the house of someone he knew. I didn't ask, because I didn't want to know. There were only so many things I could fight, and the panic attack growing inside my chest was priority. *So much blood.*

His friend took him into a back room of his house, which was set up as a small type of doctor's office. He had sterile supplies and bandages. Within thirty minutes we were in and out. Preston didn't get any type of pain medicine but given his history it made sense. He said he'd make do with something over the counter.

Once we were out of there, I insisted we go to my house. I needed to watch over him. My chest was so tight. I was struggling to breathe. Going through my mental exercises wasn't helping. I was on the verge of a full-blown anxiety attack, and I needed reassurance that Preston was going to be okay. Tonight was something out of my worst nightmare. All I could see was the blood.

We made it my house, and I quickly ushered him inside. He walked over to the couch, avoiding a collision with Sherbert, who made his irritation known at being disturbed.

"Oh, Nurse Landon. If I'm extra good, do you think maybe you can give me a sponge bath later?" Preston asked from his reclined position.

I lowered myself to my knees, trying to calm my racing heart, and examined his wound. It was covered with a white bandage, and I didn't see any blood seeping through.

"I don't know. What you did tonight was pretty dangerous. I'm not sure if you deserve one." I smiled, but I could feel the strain behind it. Preston must have seen something on my face, because his finger brushed across my cheek.

"Hey, look at me," he coaxed.

My gaze met his. *Could he see the fear and panic in my eyes?* "You could have died tonight."

"But I didn't. Because you guys were there."

My fingers gently traced the white gauze on his side. "There was so much blood." I could feel my face draining of color. There was a buzzing in my ear, and if I wasn't already almost seated, I'd probably need to sit down before I fell down.

Preston's expression was one of worry as he palmed my cheek. "Hey, talk to me. This is nothing more than a little flesh wound. I mean, it barely hurts."

I tried to smile at his attempt to lighten things up, but it was useless. He sat up and pulled me up onto the couch with him.

"Landon?"

My gaze grew unfocused as I stared straight ahead, lost

in my memories. "When I saw all the blood, all I could think about was my father."

Preston jerked but remained quiet at my side.

"I told you my parents were divorced. It happened right before I turned twelve. The whole thing was ugly and bitter. The divorce as well as the custody battle. Dad was bipolar and kept going off his meds. Mom couldn't take it anymore, so she left. After she got full custody of me, dad got back on his meds and became a productive citizen again." I laughed without humor. "The summer before my freshman year, just after I'd turned thirteen, I went to stay with him. Of course, he went off his meds again. Got depressed. I should have seen it. I mean, I'd lived with it my whole life. But I was a teenager. I didn't want to spend time at his house. I missed my friends. My mom. I just wanted to go home."

"That's understandable. Being shuttled around had to be miserable. And it's only reasonable that you'd want to spend time with your friends."

"I was such a bitch to him. Yelling all the time. Whining. Crying. I certainly didn't make things easy."

"I'm not an expert on teenage girls, but you don't sound any different than the ones I've ever encountered," he said with a small chuckle.

I sent him a small smile, but it was excruciating. I just felt so lost.

"One day, he asked me to run to the store. Grab him a pack of cigarettes. Of course, this was long before they stopped letting kids buy them. I went, but I wasn't happy about it. The entire way there and back, I thought about all the things I was going to piss and moan about after I got back."

My lower lip trembled until I caught it between my teeth.

"Have you ever walked into a place and knew that something terrible had happened in there? That little shiver that dances across the back of your neck. Or makes the hair on your arms stand on end. That's what I felt, the minute I stepped through our front door. I stood on the landing at the bottom of the stairs, and I knew."

I inhaled a shaky breath. "I knew, but still, I took one stair at a time until I reached the top. My feet kept moving, but my brain screamed for me to turn around. *Don't go any further*. I was never very good at listening. The door to my dad's room was partially shut. I can still hear the hinges squeak in my nightmares. God, there was so much blood."

"Landon, you don't have to say anymore."

I shook my head. "No, I need to tell you all of it."

I needed to keep all my emotions from exploding out of me. He'd shared his past with me. It was only fair that I did the same. I only hoped he wouldn't judge me.

"Okay," his voice trembled.

"The gun was still in his hand. I went to call 9-1-1 when I heard him say something. Or at least try to. It was so garbled, but it sounded like he said my name. I fell to my knees next to him. Slowly, like it pained him greatly, he reached for my hand. He then placed it on top of his other hand, the one that still held the gun." She sniffed back the tears that threatened to spill over. "There was so much pain in his eyes, but there was also something else. Peace. He wanted it so bad. I wanted it for him. He tried to raise the gun, but he was too weak. So, I helped him. Together our arms moved and, with a final I love you...I helped him squeeze the trigger."

A thick and heavy silence descended over us. It was so quiet I could almost hear the ticking of the clock on the kitchen wall. *Why wasn't Preston saying anything?* There was this unbearable weight of pressure on my chest making it hard to pull in a breath. Finally, he broke the silence. "That's why you were drinking that night. That's the sin you need to forgive yourself for."

Neither of those were questions, but I answered anyway.

"Yes." With that single word it was as though a weight had been lifted from my shoulders. Preston finally learned my secret. Why I didn't deserve him, even though I so desperately wanted him. Would he look at me differently, now that he knew? Cold, clammy terror snaked its way inside my belly. I was afraid to meet his eyes. Afraid of what I'd see.

A warm hand palmed my jaw and with a gentle pull, my head swiveled in his direction. My eyes locked onto the small patch of ink peeking out above the neckline of his shirt.

"Landon, look at me. Please," Preston begged.

My eyes drifted upward until my gaze met his. A spark of some emotion I was afraid to name shone from his eyes.

"You are so fucking brave. I've never met anyone as strong as you. You had the courage to help your father when he needed it the most. You amaze me. I didn't know your father, but I can only imagine that he is now at peace. Probably something he'd never experienced while on this earth." He brushed my tears off my cheeks with his thumbs. "That is the greatest gift you could have ever given him."

It was as though his words unlocked the anger, the pain, and the guilt inside me. All of those emotions culminated into a giant ball that needed to be set free. I doubled over, clutching my head. A scream exploded out of me. My scream turned into pitiful sobs, and I collapsed against

Preston's chest, burying my face against him. Everything hurt, and I expelled all the emotions I'd been bottling up inside me for the last twenty-one years.

I'd been so angry at my father for what he'd made me do. Hated him. But I couldn't do that any longer. I'd told Brody at one time that a person can do unpardonable things out of love. I'd never believed it until now. I had done it out of love. My father had suffered more than anyone I'd known, and when he couldn't end his suffering on his own, he'd asked me to help. Because he knew how strong I was.

And maybe that was an unpardonable sin. But it was a sin I could live with, because, in the end, it gave my father the peace he'd so desperately craved.

My sobs slowed. Preston's arms were wrapped so tightly around me and his whispered words finally penetrated my ears as he gently rocked me, comforting me.

"Shh, it's okay."

A hiccuped escaped, and I wiped my face with my hand. He tilted his head down and our eyes met. I scanned his face trying to read his expression. My heart jerked in my chest, and hope soared through me at what I saw. This man had pushed his way into my life. He hadn't given up on that single connection we'd had two years ago, no matter how much I tried to deny it. I couldn't deny it any longer though. Preston had worked his way into my life. Into my heart. Into the very depths of my soul.

Coming to a decision, I sat myself up, careful to avoid his wound.

"You have been this stubborn, caring man who has never given up on me, even when I gave you every reason to. Thank you for not judging me. For accepting all these ugly, insecure, and messy parts of me." I took a deep breath before letting it out. "You don't have to say anything, but I wanted you to know that I love you. I pushed you away all this time because I didn't think I deserved you. Didn't deserve to be happy. But I don't think that any longer. Not anymore."

Preston's beautiful hazel eyes lit up, and his lips twitched before shifting up into the smile I'd grown to love.

"You punished yourself for far too long. There is no one more deserving of love than you. I only hope I can give you all the love that you deserve. Because I do. Love you that is. Something about you spoke to me that night at the hotel. I think I've loved you almost from the first. Your strength and courage were present even then."

Tears of joy threatened to spill, but I blinked them back. I'd cried enough tonight. Preston leaned forward and pressed his lips to mine. He brushed them back and forth simply feeling the way our mouths moved together. He pulled back and tucked my hair behind my ear.

"Can I ask you another question about that night?" He whispered softly. "I've been wondering about it."

"Yes."

"What was with the fake name? Why Sara?"

I nervously played with the hem of my shirt. He'd learned my biggest secret. Might as well share the rest.

"I'm not sure why that name spilled out of me." I shook my head. "Actually, that's not true. I wanted to be *her* again. To become the person I was before my father's death. Sara isn't a fake name. It's real. And it's mine. Sara Landon Roberts."

Preston drew back and then reached for my hand. "What made you start going by Landon?"

"My father's death. Sara died that day too. I was no longer the same person I was before I pulled that trigger. In an instant, I changed. I grew up. Matured." I paused. "Sara had been selfish. Only thought of herself. And for one night, I wanted to be selfish again."

"Jesus. I think if anyone could be given a pass for being selfish, it's you." He brought my knuckles to his mouth and kissed each one. "Thank you for telling me. And for what it's worth, I don't think you were being selfish at all."

I smothered the yawn that appeared out of nowhere. The stress from the night was finally catching up with me. My entire body was heavy with fatigue, and I could barely move. I was enjoying his touch, though, and I didn't want it to stop. But we had a lot of plans to make tomorrow.

And despite Preston's reassurances that it was just a minor flesh wound, the truth was he'd been shot, and he surely had to be feeling the effects of it.

I cradled his cheek and gave him a final kiss before pulling back. "I love you, but we both need to get some rest."

He nodded in understanding. "I need to check in with Brody too. Let him know we're okay."

"Come to bed when you're done."

I trailed my finger down his arm and gave his hand a squeeze before heading into the bedroom to wait for him. Looking around the room, it seemed different. Preston had been in my room, my bed before, but that was before we were in love. I wasn't fighting against him or my feelings. I was fully embracing them. Feeling like a new woman, I couldn't help but smile and spin around in circle, my arms raised out to my side. This happiness was a heady feeling.

But the corners of my mouth fell as I thought about what had brought us here. Preston had been shot. He could have died tonight. That bullet could have taken him away from me. I shook my head. I couldn't think about that. He was here, and he was fine. We were going to do what we could to find out who was responsibility for supplying *Rapture*, and we were going to stop them.

"Hey, I thought you were going to bed," Preston said as he stepped into my room.

Forcing another smile to my face, I started changing into my sleep shirt and shorts. "I was just thinking."

He joined me in bed and pulled me into his uninjured side, brushing a kiss across my forehead. "I'm not sure what you were thinking about, but if the expression on your face when I walked in was anything to go by, it wasn't good."

"I'm just worried."

Preston sighed. "Me too. But we're going to get the information we need from Felipe one way or another. I promise."

I believed him. He'd been enraged yesterday after what happened to that boy Owen. There was no doubt in my mind that he'd get the information we needed. I only hoped he didn't get killed in the process.

CHAPTER 26

A STABBING PAIN WOKE ME. I twisted, trying to alleviate it, and the events of the last two days came rushing back. Who knew getting shot would hurt so damn bad? All of that went away though, because more memories of last night filtered in, and they all revolved around Landon, her secret, and finally our confession of love.

At one point in the middle of the night her mewling woke me. She'd been sweating and tangled in the sheets, moaning, tears seeping from her eyes. Her cries of pain broke my heart. Thankfully, she'd calmed at my touch and whispered words. I'd pulled her more tightly against me and although a few more whimpers escaped her, she finally quieted down. She'd remained restless the remainder of the night, and I'd barely gotten any sleep trying to soothe her.

My head tilted down, and my eyes drank in the sight of her. She wasn't a figment of my imagination. She was still here, lying in my arms. No running away this time. Her blonde hair fanned out along the pillow behind her while a chunk of it draped across her forehead and down her cheek.

Careful not to disturb her, I brushed it back, because I didn't want anything to stop me from seeing her face in the morning light.

If this was what love felt like, no wonder people were scared of it. It was terrifying knowing that this tiny woman had so much power over me. That I wanted nothing more than her happiness and the desperate urge to not disappoint her. I watched as her eyelids fluttered and then slowly opened. She'd said she loved me, but in the light of day, would she pull away? It happened every time I felt like we were moving forward. I braced myself.

"Good morning," she murmured with a sleepy smile.

"Morning," I replied a little guarded.

Her smile faded. "How are you feeling today? Is your side okay? You didn't tear open the stitches, did you?"

She quickly sat up and checked my wound over, her entire body sagging in relief to see that there was no blood seeping through the bandage. Her fingers lightly brushed my skin around it, worry etched on her face. I reached out for her hand and brought it to my lips.

"I'm okay, remember?"

Her nod was shaky as was her inhalation. "I had so many nightmares last night. I dreamed you were dead."

"Aw, Jesus. Babe, I have no intention of going anywhere. You're stuck with me."

Her bright blue eyes shimmered with wetness. "Promise?"

"I promise."

"Okay."

"Why don't you hop in the shower? I'm going to check in with the guys. See where we stand and where we're going from here."

She hesitated, as though reluctant to leave my side, but she nodded and climbed out of the bed. I crawled out of my side and headed into the living room where I'd left my phone after talking to Brody last night. I settled on the couch and dialed Victor's number.

"Hey, man, how're you feeling?"

"My side hurts like a bitch, but otherwise, I'm good. What's going on with Felipe? And what about the other three?"

"Cruz and one of the bodyguards are dead. The other one is in serious condition. A bullet nicked his liver. He made it through surgery just fine. Only problem is, he's not talking. He says he doesn't know anything about the drugs. He was just hired for muscle."

Shit. "Do you think he's telling the truth?"

"No idea. Felipe, on the other hand had some interesting things to say."

"Oh, yeah? What's that?"

"Well, after what went down last night, Brody, Pablo, and I got to talking. Your brother showed us all the surveillance footage he's managed to acquire on Elliott King and the guys you've ID'ed as Silas and Eli. So, early this morning, we took Felipe to the interrogation room and questioned him. Showed him the photos."

"And?" I asked after Victor paused.

"So impatient."

I ground my teeth. "Spit it out."

"I was about to tell you until you interrupted me."

"Victor," I bit out.

"As I was saying. It would appear that your assertation that there was no way King doesn't know what's going on in his nasty little club was correct."

I knew it. "So, how are we going to stop him?"

"That's what we've all been trying to figure out. Your brother wants us all to head to your office this afternoon so we can try and come up with a plan. Felipe is behind bars for the moment, but he lawyered up real quick when we showed him those photos. We offered a plea bargain. Right now, he has an attempted murder charge against him, in addition to the narcotics we confiscated from him last night. In exchange for more information on King, he's accepting a lesser drug charge. We're going to try and get as much out of him as we can. Names and locations."

"All right. Landon and I will meet you guys at the office. What time?"

"Brody wants everyone there at six. Pablo has also talked to his supervisor. Filled him in on everything that we've been doing. He's working on getting a warrant once we figure out where the drugs are being store and processed. He also got his ass chewed for going out on the deal last night and not getting proper back up."

I winced. "Sorry about that."

"He knew what he was getting into. In this case, he said it was worth it."

"Well, I'll have to thank him later."

"See you later tonight then."

"You got it."

I hung up and went to talk to Landon who was just stepping out of the shower.

"Did you talk to your brother?"

"No, Victor. It looks like Felipe is willing to give us King and his two guys, Silas and Eli, in exchange for them dropping the attempted murder charge. He said Brody wants to meet us at the office tonight at six so we can come up with a way to flush King out. I'm also curious to find out what other information Pablo can get out of Felipe. We still have no idea where King is storing the drugs or who he's getting them from."

"I might be able to help with that." She started getting dressed. "I'm going to head into the office and go through the data. For the last year I've been doing a lot of research on the influx of narcotics into the United States. I might be able to pinpoint a source. I can't promise any answers, but I have access to a lot of intel that might be able to help us."

I nodded. "That would be great."

Landon finished dressing and I closed the distance between us before pulling her into my arms. "I love you."

Her arms tightened around me and her lips tipped up. "Good, because I love you too."

"I couldn't have done any of this without you. I think we make a good team."

"I think we do too. I can't wait to bring these bastards down."

CHAPTER 27

I HURRIED through the hallways of the agency, shouldering my way past several people until I reached my office. While I waited for my computer to boot up, I tried calling Crawford, but it went straight to voicemail. A chirp alerted me to a new email. I scanned it quickly and then closed the program before pulling up another one. My fingers flew across the keys as I filtered through all the date the organization had been collecting over the last few months.

We had several reports from our agents in Mexico about shipments making their way to the States, but we hadn't been able to track down any of them and stop them, so they'd slipped through the cracks. A name caught my eye. *Holy shit.* I ran several more programs, siphoning information from every report. Each one pointed to a single name: *María Luisa Velasquez.*

Jesus. This was huge. I needed to get this info to Brody. I hit the print button on several pages and hurried to the office printer. Snatching the sheets out of the bin, I turned and nearly collided with a body.

"Director Gibson, I'm so sorry."

"What's the rush, Roberts?"

"I'm following up on another lead on *Rapture*, sir."

"What do you have for me?"

No way was I mentioning Brody's name.

"Last night, the local narcotics unit made an arrest. The dealer in custody gave up several names, including the man behind the entire sale of the narcotic: Elliott King. The prosecuting attorney is currently working on getting other names and locations of storage units." I gestured to the papers in my hand. "You already know about my confrontation with Mr. King. In the meantime, Crawford and Brickman started doing some digging into his financials as well as tracking purported shipments of massive quantities of cocaine that we've been unable to locate. Each shipment coincides with a withdrawal from Mr. King's bank account. And those shipments of narcotics have been linked back to a single person. *María Luisa Velasquez.*"

Gibson's eyes bulged. "Is this the same woman who took over the supply business for the Juarez Cartel after she'd killed their former supplier, Raúl Escobar? Emilio Salazar's younger half-sister?"

I nodded emphatically. "Yes, sir, one and the same."

"Jesus." He ran a hand through his hair.

"Once I locate where King is storing and cutting the cocaine, we'll need to assemble a team to prepare for seizure."

"I'll talk to one of the Federal judges and get him on standby for a warrant the minute you can give me probable cause. Keep me appraised of the situation, Roberts."

"Yes, sir."

He continued on his way down the hall toward his office.

Excitement buzzed through my veins. This is what I'd missed being stuck behind a computer for the last year. I hustled back to my office, grabbed my stuff, and raced out the door. I'd try and reach Crawford on my way to Preston and Brody's office. I couldn't wait to tell the guys what I'd found.

~

"So, I did some digging today and you guys aren't going to believe what I came up with." My leg bounced with the rush of adrenaline. I'd finally gotten a hold of Crawford. He was going to talk to Brickman, and they'd be ready for whatever the plan was. Now we just had to come up with it.

Brody and Preston exchanged glances of anticipation. "Tell us what you got."

"María Luisa Velasquez is most likely the one supplying Mr. King with his cocaine. There have been reports of missing drug shipments coming in from Mexico. It's as though they've just disappeared. Somehow they're managing to sneak them into the country. Oh," I held up the data I'd printed off. "I also discovered that Mr. King has been making extremely large withdrawals around the same time those cocaine shipments have gone missing. And, I finally got the chemical analysis of what is being used to cut *Rapture*. Normally, only one cutting agent is used, but it would seem that King is using a combination of two. Laundry detergent and Levamisole. Both of those are common cutting agents in and of themselves, but you start mixing them, and…"

Brody held up his hand. "Are you sure? About Velasquez, I mean."

"Almost one hundred percent, why?"

He didn't answer. Instead, he began digging through the files and papers strewn about his desk. Preston and I watched him with bated breath. "Ah, here." He yanked a piece of paper out of the stack. "Do you have the dates of those missing shipments?"

I scanned my paperwork. "The first one was September 24, the second November 13, and it looks like the most recent one was--"

"January 8?" Brody interrupted.

My head jerked up, and I met his eyes. "Yes."

"That coincides with incoming shipments of beer and alcohol to the local delivery company that King owns."

"Wait a minute," I told him trying to wrap my head around this. "Are you thinking that the cocaine is getting smuggled into the country with the beer and alcohol shipments and then transported to King's delivery service warehouse?"

"It would make it easy. He has a large warehouse where the delivery trucks are housed at night. He can have the drugs taken off the supply trucks and put somewhere else so no one misses them."

"But that means he'd have to have people on the inside of his warehouse taking those specific crates off the trucks and moving them elsewhere," I stated.

Preston spoke up. "My bet is on Silas and Eli. They could be the inside men. They'd have knowledge of the drug arrivals. King could make sure that they were scheduled to work the day those particular shipments arrived. If they're the ones unloading the truck and taking inventory of the stock, they could easily remove those crates and hide them elsewhere. It's also not a stretch that they would be the ones in charge of the cutting operation and then distributing it to Felipe and Cruz. "

What he said made a lot of sense, but that meant King was taking a huge risk. "Do we really think that a man as smart as King is going to have a whole drug cutting process right in his own warehouse?"

"I think a man who believes no one can touch him would have his entire business in his own warehouse." Brody pointed out. "Besides, I've taken a look at his businesses. The building is huge. The deliveries are made at night. The trucks are unloaded and placed in refrigeration units. The next morning, the delivery trucks are loaded with the beer and alcohol and delivered to King's various clubs and restaurants. Then, the drivers park their trucks at night and go home. No one wanders around inside. It's in and out. Which means it's the perfect place to house a cutting lab. I honestly think it's worth checking out."

"When I talked to Victor earlier, he said that according to Felipe, he meets with Silas and Eli at the warehouse every time to make their exchange. Their supply stock up is supposed to be two days from now." Preston explained.

I looked at Brody. "I talked to Gibson. He's ready to get us the team we need to raid King's facility, but we have to have the confirmation that the drugs are there. He's going to contact a judge for a warrant as soon as we call."

His expression was serious. "After all this, I think we definitely have enough even circumstantial evidence to prove probable cause. Give him a call and see if you can get that warrant.

Despite the tension in the room, Preston smirked. "I guess *now* we get to go on that field trip?"

CHAPTER 28

"YOU'RE KIDDING, right? Did the judge seriously deny the warrant?" I stared at Landon in disbelief. Brody paced the room with a disgusted grumble.

She shook her head, her anger nearly palpable. "It's such bullshit. Apparently he said there wasn't enough evidence to indicate that the amount of cocaine in question justified sending in an entire team of DEA agents. Said it was better left up to Chicago PD and their narcotics unit."

"Son of a bitch." Brody slammed his palms down on his desktop.

My anger was just as fierce as my brother's, but his was quicker to fire. I tapped my pen on my desk. There had to be something. I jerked upright and the pen fell out of my fingers. "Wait a minute. Victor said that Pablo had already given his supervisor a heads up, and that they could get us a warrant as soon as we got a hit on where the drugs were being stored." I spread my hands out. "Well, now we have a location."

Brody wagged his finger. "You're right. Shit, let me call him and see if he can work some magic. It'll take a lot less time to get a warrant through the District Attorney's office than through Federal channels anyway."

While he made his phone call, I moved to where Landon was sitting. I pulled over the other office chair and sat next to her. I cradled her hands in mine. "How are you doing? You haven't gotten much sleep over the past couple nights."

"I should be asking you that question. Is your side okay?"

I waved off her concern. "I promise I'll let you know if it's bothering me. How's that?"

She tilted her chin in that stubborn way of hers, but finally she relented. "You better."

I leaned up and pressed my lips to hers. She was running on fumes. We all were. This would all be over soon though. It had to be.

"Good news," Brody interrupted. "I hope anyway. Pablo talked to his supervisor in the narcotics division and after sharing all our evidence to the district attorney, he's pretty sure we'll get a warrant. In the next couple hours, if we're lucky. Until then, there's not much we can do."

I glanced over at him. "What happens if he can't get the warrant?"

My brother rubbed his hands over his face. "Then we'll have to keep searching for more evidence. We may even have to confront King. Let him know we're on to him. Try and force him to do something. Whether it's move his drugs to a new location or something else."

"Well, then we better hope Pablo gets that warrant."

Brody eyed the two of us. "Both of you look exhausted. Why don't you go home and catch some sleep. If we get this warrant, then it's going to be a long night."

My brother was right. While we might not be involved in the actual seizure, we were going to make sure Pablo made it home safe and sound. Ines had already had one brother die in the line of duty, she and the rest of the family would have difficulty making it if they lost another. Plus, Victor would be with us. There was no way he was staying home while we were all out there. The one thing about the Rodriguez family, they were there for each other, no matter what.

I stood from my chair and pulled Landon with me. "Call us when you hear something."

Brody nodded. "Will do."

We took my car back to Landon's house. She leaning against the window, and I could see her eyelids growing heavy. Once I parked, I helped her out of the car and inside. We headed straight to the bedroom where we both undressed and fell onto the bed, our energy completely depleted. Fatigue overcame us, and we were oblivious to the outside world.

I WAS JERKED AWAKE BY THE RINGING PHONE. BLINDLY reaching for it, I managed to grab it and swipe across the screen. Landon stirred beside me. "Hello?" It came out on a croak.

"It's Pablo. I got the warrant, and we have a team lined up and ready to head to the warehouse."

I shot upright in bed. "Seriously?"

"Yes."

I pulled the phone away from my mouth. "They got the warrant."

Pablo was talking again. "I talked to Victor. I'm not going

to try and persuade you guys to stay home, because I'd be wasting my breath. Just stay far enough away, and don't let anyone see you."

"Of course. You be fucking careful in there. We don't know who you're going to be up against."

"I will. Alright, I got to go. You be careful as well, and I'll catch you all later."

I tossed my phone on the nightstand. "They're getting ready to head over there. Victor, Brody, and I are going to stay close to keep an eye on Pablo."

Landon pushed herself upright and glared at me. "I know you're not suggesting that I stay here?"

"I can't worry about you and Pablo, too."

She crossed her arms over her chest. "You did not just say that. I've been on countless narcotic seizures over the last seven years. You've been a PI for what, two months? And you just got fucking shot two days ago. Fuck that. I should be the one worried about you. Don't you trust me to watch your back?"

Despite her anger, I also heard the hurt behind her question. Shit. "Hey, come here."

I tugged her arm and pulled her onto my lap. Her bright blue eyes shimmered. I tucked her hair behind her ear. "There's no one I trust more."

She huffed and wrapped her arms around my neck. "Then why didn't you say that?"

With a single move, I flipped us so she was lying on her back and my body caged hers. She squealed in surprise. "I don't trust you to just watch my back. I trust you with everything. My back. My front."

I placed one of her hands over my heart, holding it there. I whispered softly. "I trust you with my life. With my heart."

Lowering my head, I covered her lips with mine. I put all my love into the kiss, showing her exactly how I felt. If only we had time to make love, but we needed to get moving. "I'm tabling this for later tonight, after we put away some drug dealers. Be ready."

She snorted. "Oh, I'll be ready. Now, let's go."

Brody called as we were about to head out the door. "Pablo call you?"

"Yes. We were about to head out the door."

"Don't bother. Victor and I are on our way over there to pick you up. ETA ten minutes."

"Guess we'll see you in a few."

I didn't get a response, because he'd already hung up.

"The cavalry is on their way. Be here soon."

"I'll be ready."

My curiosity was peeked watching her dig around in her closet. *What was she looking for?* She stood and turned, and I got my answer. In Landon's hand was a gun. She checked her ammunition and slung the holster over her shoulders. Seeing her armed was actually a huge fucking turn on, and I couldn't stop the grin from spreading across my face.

"What?" She sent me a confused glare.

"Nothing. I've just never seen you wearing a gun before. It's pretty hot."

Landon rolled her eyes. "Oh my god."

She rammed her shoulder into me as she passed, and I fake stumbled. "Maybe later you can pull out your hand-cuffs. You do have a pair, don't you?"

I waggled my eyebrows drawing a burst of laughter from her. "Come on, Romeo. Your brother should be here any minute."

Sure enough, we reached the living room, and the bell

rang. Landon opened the door. Brody glanced between the two of us. "Let's do this."

CHAPTER 29

PRESTON and I were seated in the back. It was a little surreal to be heading to a drug seizure with Brody and not actually being the ones doing the arresting. If my father could see me now. Regardless of all his faults, and how awful I'd treated him after the divorce, he'd always been proud of me. He'd told me how smart I was and how far in life I was going to go. I wish he could have been here to see this moment. Hell, to see me fall in love. My eyes took a quick glance upward. *Maybe he was.*

Out of the corner of my eye, I saw Preston watching me. I turned to him with a reassuring smile and grabbed his hand, pulling it into my lap. There was a heavy tension in the car. No one spoke, but we were all alert and observing our surroundings. Especially as Brody slowed the car. He cut the headlights and pulled as near as he could to the warehouse where we wouldn't be spotted. Next, he cut the engine, and we all watched Pablo and his team swarm the front of the building like little ants. If not for the full moon and the flashlights they carried, I didn't think we'd have been able to see them.

We couldn't hear from this distance, but I saw someone pound on the door and his mouth moved. There was a short pause where nothing happened. *Maybe nobody was inside.* No sooner had the thought crossed my mind than madness erupted in the form of gunfire.

On instinct, I reached for the door handle, ready to dive out of the car and rush over there.

"No," Preston and Brody both hollered.

"Stay put." Brody tempered his voice. "We can't go rushing in there. It will only distract them and put us at risk."

Fuck. I sank back into the seat. That was Victor's brother. He had to be going insane. I sat behind him, so I couldn't see his face, but his shoulders were rigid. Then, through the crack between his seat and the paneling that divided the front seat from the back, I caught a glimpse of his fingers digging deep into his door's arm rest. Sitting here must be torture for him.

My eyes returned to the scene. The front door of the warehouse had been busted open and all the police were squeezing through the entrance. Pablo was nowhere in sight. The side windows of the car were beginning to fog up from the heat of our breath, but no one bothered to swipe it off.

We could see flashes of light burst one after another through the warehouse windows. Long minutes passed until they gradually wound down. Brody turned the key in the ignition a half turn and cracked his window. We all craned our heads and strained to hear, but there was only the slight breeze. The window slid back up. The faint sound of sirens grew louder, flashing red and white lights lit up the sky around us and fire trucks, cop cars, and an ambulance rolled past us and into the parking lot of the warehouse. EMTs jumped out and raced inside the building.

A blaring ring from a phone scared the shit out of me, and I almost jumped out of my skin. It was Victor's.

"Hello?"

Pause.

"Motherfuck…"

Another pause.

"I'll be right there."

He stabbed his finger against the phone screen. I glanced at Preston and then, boom, Victor punched the dashboard.

Brody tried to calm him down. "Hey, talk to us, man. What's going on? What happened? Victor, you have to breathe. Come on, you can do it."

With ragged, gasping breaths, he finally settled back into his seat. "I have to go in there."

"Okay," Brody assured him. "But tell us what happened first."

"Pablo took a bullet."

I smothered a gasp while Preston and Brody cursed.

"He's alive. That's all I know."

"Go. Make sure he's okay. Call us when you find anything out."

Victor nodded absently, but he was already halfway out the door. I watched him take off at a clip toward the building, eventually slowing with his hands up as an officer from one of the cruisers spun on him. They spoke for a minute and then Victor disappeared inside the building.

"There's nothing more we can do." Brody started up the car and drove us away from the scene.

Preston squeezed my hand. I returned the gesture with a

faint smile. The next time I blinked, we were in front of my house. *We were here already?* He helped me out of the car and leaned down to speak softly to his brother. So softly, I couldn't make out what he said. Brody cast a quick glance in my direction before returning Preston's gaze. He gave him a single nod before he pulled away from the curb.

Hand in hand, we headed into the house. After the first time I'd had trouble putting the key in the lock, because my hands shook so bad, Preston took them from me and let us in. Sherbert greeted us with his standard chirp, and I picked him up to cuddle him against my chest. His purr revved louder, and my body shook with it.

"Landon, baby, it's okay. Pablo is going to be fine."

My head jerked up, and Preston was nothing but a blur. *Why did my chest hurt so bad?* Sherbert let out a small yowl and scrambled out of my grasp to drop to the floor. Then the floodgates opened. I couldn't breathe. Only sob. Strong arms wrapped around me and the smell of spring and sunshine penetrated my senses. I clutched Preston to me, my fingers gripping him so hard my knuckles hurt.

He scooped me up, and I had a vague awareness of him carrying me down the hall. The lights stayed off, and he gently laid me on the bed before crawling in next to me as my tears drenched his shirt. All night he held me as my cries raged on, whisper reassurances until eventually, with a hiccup, I fell into an exhausted sleep.

CHAPTER 30

IT HAD BEEN three days since the bust at King's delivery company. As suspected, an entire cutting lab had been located inside the facility behind state-of-the-art security. At least three skids of pure cocaine worth millions of dollars had been confiscated. There'd been enough there that the D.E.A. had been officially called in. Landon's co-workers, Crawford and Brickman had shown up along with a few other agents.

Silas and Eli had been killed, and King had disappeared without a trace. Pablo was still in the hospital, but he was being released tomorrow. He'd taken a bullet to the leg, directly above the knee, breaking his femur. He'd had to have surgery and wasn't going to be able to put any weight on it for however many weeks until it healed.

Landon had taken the last couple days off work. She'd called her therapist and I'd taken her in for her session the day after the raid. After she'd come out, her eyes had been red and swollen and she'd been quiet. We didn't talk about her reaction to what happened. I'm not sure even she knew what had triggered it. Instead, we'd spent a lot of time on the couch with her in my arms.

I'd come into the office this morning, and she said she was feeling well enough to get out of the house later. She promised to go out to lunch with me. Which meant she would be here any minute.

"So, how does it feel to be a big hero?" I leaned back with my arms crossed behind my head and a shit-eating grin on my face.

Brody shot me the finger. "Fuck off."

"You were the one who discovered the coinciding shipments and had the bright idea that King was getting and keeping his shit in that warehouse of his. I guess it's true that you got the brains and I got the beauty in the family."

"You're such a dick. You know that, right? I still can't figure out what the hell Landon sees in you."

"My charm is undeniable, what can I say?"

Brody just shook his head.

"Speaking of my lady love, she should be on her way over her soon. We're grabbing something for lunch. Do you want us to bring you back anything?"

" Where are you guys going?"

"I was thinking about this Italian...oh, here she is. Hey ba—" My mouth snapped closed and the word broke off.

"Fuck," Brody whispered beneath his breath.

"You." Spittle flew from Elliott King's mouth as that single word came out as a curse. In his hand was a gun, and he waved it back and forth between my brother and me. He stepped further into the office, closing the door behind him. "This is all your fault. The both of you have ruined everything."

Normally a well-put together man in his designer suits

with his salt and pepper hair perfectly sculpted with pomade and his wingtip shoes polished to a high shine, but not this version of him. This King's hair stood on end in several places as though he'd been running his hands through it. His suit jacket was unbuttoned, and the starched white dress shirt was half untucked. His shoes were scuffed and his chin was covered in three days growth.

"Mr. King," Brody spoke calmly. "You need to put the gun down."

I needed to draw his attention away from my brother so he could reach for the gun he kept secured under the desk. King was not a stable man. His eyes were wild and crazed as he darted glances back and forth between Brody and me.

"Shut up," he screamed. "Just shut up. Do you have any idea what you two have done? I was making millions. For what? To have some dope fiend decide he's found God and come in and destroy what I've worked hard for?"

King paced, his gun still trained on us. I'd been shot once already. I had no desire for it to happen again.

"Everything was going so perfectly. It was a win-win for everyone."

I couldn't take it any longer. "No one was winning but you, asshole. Your shit product was killing people. Kids. You were making money while sons, daughters, sisters, and brothers were dying. Fuck you."

King sneered and swung the gun back in my direction just as the door opened.

"Honey, I'm—" Landon froze.

It all seemed to happen in slow motion. My heart stopped in my chest. King pivoted in Landon's direction. The gun pointed straight at her. Brody jerked his 9mm out from under the desk. Pulled the trigger. Landon screamed, and I lurched from behind my desk to race over to her. King was writhing and moaning in pain on the floor, clutching his leg, blood pooling beneath him. Brody kicked the gun away that had fallen to the floor. He then ripped his shirt off over his head.

"I need to try and stop the bleeding. Call an ambulance."

"You okay?" I asked Landon who frantically nodded her head.

"I'm fine. Go." She pushed me away and then went to help Brody.

I made the call while I watched the two of them wrap the shirt around King's leg to try and stop the bleeding. Jesus, there was a lot of blood.

"The paramedics are on their way," I told them. "How's he doing?"

Brody shook his head. "Not good. The bullet must have nicked an artery. I'm trying to put as much pressure on it as I can, but he's losing a lot of blood."

I let the two of them do whatever they needed to do and stayed out of their way. Finally, the paramedics and firemen showed up and they got King loaded onto a stretcher and taken away. He'd long since lost consciousness. Things didn't look good for him. Within a few minutes the police arrived. I collapsed into my chair and tugged Landon down into it with me. Leaving Brody to deal with the cops was probably a shitty thing to do, but my heart was still racing even with my woman safely in my arms.

"When you walked through that door, I swear to god my heart stopped. I thought he was going to shoot you. He was out of his mind with rage."

Landon's arms tightened around my neck and she raised her head from my shoulder. "But he didn't. We're both okay."

I glanced over at Brody. "Do you think King's going to make it?"

"It's hard to say. He was losing an awful lot of blood. I guess we'll have to wait and see."

Finally the police left and Brody joined us.

"They took my statement and are going to let me know how King is once they find out. If he pulls through, he'll be under arrest."

A breath of air left my lungs. I couldn't believe it. We'd actually managed to take down an entire drug ring. It was completely unimaginable.

"Why don't you two get out of here. I'm going to take the rest of the day off. I need to see Ines."

Once again he rose from his chair and grabbed his coat without another word. I couldn't imagine how Brody was feeling right now. He'd just shot a man. One who could die. That was a lot of responsibility to take on. It wouldn't be the first man he'd killed, but over the last year I'd learned a lot about my brother. He did what needed to be done and made no apologies for it. Still, it must weigh on him. It made me glad he had Ines. She loved his broody ass, flaws and all. And she'd take care of him. My eyes shifted to the woman in my lap. The woman I loved more than anything. I needed to take care of her.

I tightened my grip on her hips. That same electrical charged surged through my fingertips every time I touched her. "Come on, let's go home. It's finally over."

CHAPTER 31

Four months later

The trees were in full bloom. Flowers dotted the shores of the lake, sprinkling a myriad of colors as far as the eye could see. The aroma of spring and sunshine was all around me. It had become my favorite scent. It reminded me of rebirth and new beginnings. Two things I never thought I'd be thankful for. I stood on the flat rock platform and inhaled the sweet smell. Warm hands wrapped around my waist, and I smiled, covering them with my own. I tilted my head to give him better access to press soft kisses along my neck.

"Hello, beautiful," Preston whispered in my ear.

I leaned back into his embrace. "Hi."

There was the sound of birds singing and the occasional frog croaking. I could hear the low buzz of other conversations around us, but no one but Preston and I mattered in this tiny oasis.

"How's the baby?"

"Oh my god, Landon. She's the most perfect thing I've seen. Didn't even fuss the whole time I was there. I swear she smiled at me."

"I've heard babies smile when they're gassy."

"Hey, now." Preston tickled my side, and I squirmed and giggled in his arms. I turned so we were face to face and wrapped my arms around his neck. He was smiling down at me, his hazel eyes glowing with affection.

"I wish I'd been able to go with you. I wanted to see her again, but I had to go out with Brickman and Crawford on that seize."

"Neither of you are going anywhere. If you want, we can go see her tomorrow."

"You sure Ines wouldn't mind?"

"You're Zoey's aunt. And I know Ines really wants to become friends. She told me to tell you she'd be happy for you to come by anytime."

This new life was so different. I actually had friends. A family. A new niece. Although, she wasn't technically family since Preston and I weren't married.

"You've got that weird look on your face."

I narrowed my eyes. "What weird look?"

"That look that says you're not sure this is all real."

"Sometimes I wonder that it is. Do you know that I dreamt about us in this place once?"

Preston raised a brow. "What was the dream about?"

"I was standing here, just like this, looking out over the water. A man, you, came up behind me and wrapped me in your arms like you did just now. You just held me. Protected me. It was the first time since my father's death that I'd felt peace."

"What about now? Do you still feel that peace?"

I smiled up at him. Every day with Preston brought me more and more.

"Only with you."

"I love you. I hope you know that."

"How could I not? You show me every day just how much. I love you, too."

As though in slow motion, Preston lowered himself to the ground and reached out for my hands. My breath lodged in my chest.

"Sara Landon Roberts, you've brought me more happiness than I could ever have imagined. You've taught me about strength and courage. You've also taught me about forgiveness. I don't think I've brought you as much peace as you've brought me. You quiet the chaos inside my head. You love me for all my faults, which we both know there are plenty. You make me a better man. I love you with all that I have."

Preston releases my hands, and reached into his pocket, pulling out a small, square box. Inside was the most beautiful diamond ring. He reached for my left hand and spoke as he slid the ring down my finger. "Will you marry me?"

"Yes." I was nodding before he'd even finished his question. "Yes."

He rose and our lips met in a fierce kiss. Shouts and clapping surrounded us, but I didn't pay it any attention. My whole focus was on this man who, despite all the hell I'd put him through, loved me. He broke the kiss and laid his forehead against mine.

"Thank god, you put this poor bastard out of his misery."

Preston laughed, and we both turned to see Victor and Estelle, who was just barely beginning to show signs of early pregnancy, standing at the top of the rock steps. They both made their way down to us. Estelle gave me a hug, something I was still getting used to. Lord, this family was a bunch of huggers. "Congratulations, Landon. I'm so happy for you both."

Victor and Preston hugged it out bro style with an across the body handshake with chest bump and a single pat on the back. Everyone switched and I was also subject to a short and simple hug from Victor. Being a part of a family was something I was going to have to get used to. It was definitely going to take some time.

"It's supposed to be a surprise, but my dad is throwing you guys an impromptu engagement party. We're supposed to find some way to get you guys over to the house. The rest of the family, including Brody, Ines, and Zoey, will all be there. So, when we get there, can you please act surprised?"

"You mean, like, right now?" My voice squeaked.

"Yes, right now. He's so excited to be gaining another daughter, he couldn't wait to celebrate."

My mind was whirling. I didn't know what to say. Panic was beginning to build.

"Hey, will you guys give us a second, please?" Preston asked.

Victor and Estelle's expressions shifted to nervousness. "Oh, sorry, yeah, of course."

He pulled me into his arms and instantly I calmed. The engagement and now the party, it was all so overwhelming. Preston didn't let go of me, but he pulled back enough to look at me.

"You okay, now?"

I nodded. "I think so."

"We don't have to go. Ernesto will understand. Suddenly

being part of this huge family is a lot to take in. Believe me, I know."

"It's all just happening so fast."

"Then we'll slow it down. It's okay."

I laid my head on Preston's chest, soaking in his heat. His scent. His strength. I could do this. These people were my family now. They loved and they loved hard. This man had taught me so much about courage. I wasn't that person anymore. The one who was always afraid to let people love me. I pulled back.

"No, let's go."

He stared down at me with those hazel eyes I loved so much. "Are you sure?"

I smiled up at him. "Definitely. I'm sure Ernesto has worked hard to do something nice for us. And this is our family."

"I love you."

"I love you, too."

We turned to Victor and Estelle who stood there, uncertainly. "How's this look for my surprised face?"

I made my eyes bulge and my mouth formed into the shape of an 'O' at the same time I covered my cheeks with my hands. Everyone grimaced and then burst out laughing. Preston wrapped his arm around my waist and tugged me into his side. "Come on. We'll work on it in the car."

The four of us headed up the stairs and along the grassy path. I cast one final glance over my shoulder at the lake and marveled at the beauty of it. I didn't need a magical snow globe. I only needed love.

EPILOGUE

"Mommy, I hold baby?" Maisie bounced around in her car seat in the back with the exuberance of a typical three-year old.

"We'll have to ask Ms. Ines, sweetie. You'll have to be really careful. Babies are fragile and we have to be gentle with them."

"I promise, I be gentle," she said solemnly.

My heart ached a little at how serious she'd quickly become. Unfortunately, Maisie had learned at an early age how harmful people could be if they weren't gentle. Pushing away the bad memories, I smiled at her reflection in the rearview mirror.

We pulled in front of the blue ranch style house that sat in a quiet neighborhood. This was the kind of area I dreamed of living in. Good schools. Children playing with each other in their yards. Friends having other friends over for a cook-out. A peaceful place to raise your kids.

I helped Maisie out of her car-seat and we walked hand in hand up the sidewalk. I glanced around with a heavy heart.

Sadly, I'd never live in a neighborhood like this. All that was in my future, Maisie's future, was a small, one-bedroom apartment in a rundown building. Where, instead of children's laughter outside, gunshots and sirens were the background noise of daily living. People screaming at each other.

Instead of the smell of freshly cut grass, it was the acrid scent of garbage and the skunky scent of weed filling the hallway from someone smoking three doors down.

A glowing Latina woman stepped out of the house. "Michele, I'm so glad you came. Come in. Brody is just changing Zoey's diaper."

Once we were inside, she squatted down to my daughter's level, and pulled her into a hug. "Hi, Maisie May. I'm so happy to see you again. I've missed you."

"I hold baby?"

I laughed self-consciously. "Sorry, she's been asking me that ever since I said we were coming over here to meet her. I told her we'd have to see."

She stayed where she was and spoke gently to my daughter. "You'll have to sit in a chair and someone will have to help you a little, but you can definitely hold the baby."

"Thank you. I hold baby."

Ines rose and we both laughed. "Come on, let's go have a seat. Brody should be out any minute. Oh, my brother Pablo is supposed to stop over sometime too, but not sure when."

He and Manuel were the only two of Ines' family member's I hadn't met yet. I knew Victor, and I'd only by chance met her father one time.

"Michele, it's good to see you."

I glanced up to see Brody step into the living room with a

small bundle in his arms. Maisie started clapping her hands and jumping up and down excitedly. "Hi baby. I see her? Pretty please?" She turned to me with the most pitiful expression. "Please, mommy?" She drew out the please in the most adorable and begging way.

I looked helplessly at Ines, who was smiling brightly. Brody thankfully responded for me. "Come on, baby girl."

Maisie popped her hands on her hips like the little diva she was. "I not a baby. I a big girl."

He covered his chest with his free hand. "Of course you're a big girl. Only big girls get to hold the baby."

In awe, I watched as this giant of a man took my daughter's hand and led her over to the couch. He helped her crawl up in the corner, and grabbed a pillow. It was the sweetest thing to see Brody situating little Zoey in Maisie's arms. With the utmost patience, he showed her just the right way to place her arms, gently guiding and instructing her to support the baby's head.

"She's doing a great job, Michele. I think you have a natural on your hands. They'll be fine. Let's go in the kitchen and catch up. I feel like I haven't seen you in forever. You need to tell me how things are going with school and how all the girls are doing at the club."

For the next hour, Ines and I sat and talked. Sometime during our visit, Brody popped in with Zoey and said that all the excitement must have been too much for Maisie, and she'd fallen asleep on the couch. He'd gone and also put the baby down for a nap. But now it was time for me to go. I needed to get Maisie to the sitter's so I could study a little bit before heading to my shift at *Sweet SINoritas*. Only a few more months, and I would be free of that place.

"Thank you for your patience with Maisie. She gets a little excited."

Ines hugged me. "She's absolutely adorable. I hope you guys can stop by again soon. It'll be nice to have another kid around. Gives us an idea of what to look forward to."

I couldn't help but both laugh and feel sorry for them. Especially during the terrible twos. "You and Brody are going to do great."

"We'll have to ask you for some pointers. You're an amazing mom and Maisie is so lucky to have you."

My throat tightened and my eyes burned. "Thank you."

Being a single mother was the hardest thing I'd ever done in my life. I'd screwed up so many times. And I was so fucking tired. I followed Ines into the living room just as the front door opened and a tall, dark haired man stepped through.

"Pablo," Ines stage whispered excitedly, keeping her voice down since Maisie was sleeping. She quickly hugged her brother and he gingerly took a few steps, a small limp noticeable in his stride. There was a pinch of guilt seeing that limp.

"Hey sis," he greeted her. "Zoey sleeping?"

My head jerked up, and a shiver skated across my skin at his voice. Honey-colored eyes stared down at me. His dark, shaggy hair fell across a broad forehead and curled up at the edge of his collar and around his ears. He probably needed a haircut, but I'd kill anyone who took scissors to it. *Whoa, where did that come from?*

"Brody laid her down for a nap about fifteen minutes ago. If you're quiet though, you can probably peek in on her. Oh," she smacked her forehead. "I don't think you two have ever actually met. Pablo, this is my friend, Michele. Michele, my brother."

"Hi. Um, Ines told me you were shot while trying to find out who was behind *Rapture*. I'm really sorry. I feel I'm partially to blame. If I hadn't come to Brody and Preston, maybe that wouldn't have happened. Anyway, I'm really sorry." I snapped my mouth shut.

He smiled, but something about it seemed strained. *Shit, he probably blamed me.*

"It's not your fault. Hazard of the job."

I cleared my throat. "Still, I'm really sorry. Anyway, I should get going. I have to drop Maisie off at the sitter's."

Scooping up my daughter, I heaved her up to a position where I had a good grip on her.

"Would you like some help?" Pablo asked.

For a moment I hesitated, but even as small as Maisie was, dead weight made it difficult to pull open a car door and also to try and situate her in the car seat. I bit my lip. "Are you sure?"

"Of course, she probably gets heavy."

He gently took her from my arms and held her tenderly against his chest. I turned to hug Ines. "Thank you again for letting us come by and see Zoey. It was the highlight of Maisie's day."

"You know you're always welcome to come over. I've missed you."

"Same here." I waved goodbye and led Pablo out to the car. Ever so gently, he laid her in her car seat and buckled her in.

"Thank you."

He inclined his head. "You're welcome."

His eyes stayed locked on me, and I stood there awkwardly, not sure what to say. He didn't seem angry, but something about him intimidated me. "Um, I should get going. Thanks again."

I dashed into the driver's seat and slowly backed out of the driveway, checking both directions before pulling out into the road. Pablo never moved. He continued watching me. Not in a creepy way, but as though he couldn't *not* look at me. Our arms had touched as I transferred Maisie into his grasp, and his honey-colored eyes had darkened. Long after I left him standing in Ines' driveway, I could feel my skin burn.

It didn't matter, because chances were, despite my friendship with his sister, I'd probably never see him again. *Why did that make me sad?*

Thank you so much for reading ATONEMENT! I hope you enjoyed it. If so, I'd greatly appreciate a review on the platform of your choice. Reviews are so important!

Pablo and Michele's story will be coming in 2021!
Be sure to sign up for my newsletter to stay up to date on details! http://bit.ly/LKShawNewsletter

Want to see how Brody and Ines got together?
Be sure to check out IN TOO DEEP!
Get your copy here: https://amzn.to/2O8pETl

What about Victor and Estelle?
You can read about them in STRIKING DISTANCE
Get your copy here: https://amzn.to/2Ct8f1h

If you enjoyed the LOVE UNDERCOVER series, then you'll
LOVE the DOMS OF CLUB EDEN!
Start the best-selling series today with SUBMISSION.
FREE with Kindle Unlimited!
Amazon: https://amzn.to/2WeWvHv

Turn the page for a peek at Submission, Book 1.

SUBMISSION

"You can do this," I muttered to myself while I peeped out my car windshield. With a deep exhale, I wiped my sweaty palms on my pant leg and tried to calm the butterflies in my belly. I could feel my heart beating in my ears. I'd been sitting here for thirty minutes. I looked down at the ridiculous container of store-bought potato salad. It was probably getting warm. And gross.

I caught movement out of my periphery. Just a couple walking to their car. I didn't know what I hoped to see from my parking space way in the back. The longer I sat there, though, the greater the urge was to leave. But damn it, I'd come this far. What could it hurt to mingle a little? I mean, these were just normal people, right? Kinky people, but still totally normal. Except for me. I was as vanilla as they came. Or was I? That's what I was here to find out.

Now or never. With that, I quickly grabbed the stupid plastic tub and exited my car before I changed my mind. With a determined stride, I made my way across the parking lot and up the sidewalk toward the shelter house. My steps stuttered briefly when heads turned at my entrance. I gave an awkward smile and set my offering in an empty space between a tin pan of burnt hot dogs and a mostly empty baking dish of what looked like macaroni and cheese.

When I turned back around, no one was paying me any attention. Trying to remain inconspicuous, I stepped off to the side to stand against the wall, observing those sitting at the picnic tables scattered around.

"Well, who do we have here?" A deep, gravelly voice at my right drew my attention. My breath hitched and my body heated when I spotted the sexiest man I'd ever laid eyes on. I'd always been a sucker for a man with salt and pepper hair. Damn, he filled out that navy t-shirt nicely. My eyes traveled his full length before returning to his face. I flushed at the amused half-smile he wore at my perusal. It took me a moment to remember he'd asked me a question.

"Pe-Penny," I stuttered, almost breathless as the heat in my face intensified. I don't remember blushing this much before in my life. *Fake it 'til you make it* was my mantra. I stood a little taller and attempted to gain the confidence I typically displayed with chauvinistic surgeons.

"I'm Marcus." His secret smile remained as he reached out to shake my hand. When I placed mine in his, he squeezed it firmly, and I thought I felt his thumb gently caress mine, but he pulled away before I could be sure.

"Nice to meet you." The words came out a little shaky.

"So, what brings you out to play with us today?" His voice dropped suggestively.

Maintaining my barely-there confidence, I answered his question. "I'm curious about domination and submission. I figured this was the best place to gain some knowledge."

"Knowledge about what?" Marcus asked, showing true interest.

Everything. I wanted to know what it felt like to give up control.

To just feel and not have to think.

To be dominated.

To have someone fulfill needs I didn't even know I had.

I wanted to find my happily ever after, damn it. Sadly, I didn't know how to express any of this.

I shrugged my shoulders. "Whatever someone will teach me."

"Sweetness," he murmured, "I'd be happy to teach you anything you want to know. In the meantime, why don't I introduce you to some friends of mine."

With a hand across my lower back, startling me with the sparks of electricity that flowed through my extremities, Marcus led me over to a group of women.

"Ladies, I'd like to introduce you to Penny. This is her first munch. She's here getting the lay of the land, so to speak. I have no doubt you'll make her feel welcome." There was an undercurrent of command in his tone.

I sat on the bench and Marcus moved away. The back of my neck tingled like I was still being watched, but I ignored the sensation.

"Hi, I'm Bridget."

My eyes landed on a gorgeous redhead with chocolate-colored eyes and a bright, welcoming smile that seemed genuine. She looked about my age. She continued introducing the rest of the group while she pointed at each woman who waved when she spoke their name. "That's Delilah, Jackie, and Priscilla, but we call her Priss."

"Nice to meet you."

"Soooo," she drew out the word, "I assume you're a sub?"

"Um, I'm not really sure."

She laughed. "Well, if you're not, then Marcus there is going to be sadly disappointed."

My face heated.

"He hasn't taken his eyes off you since the moment you sat down." This came from Delilah.

"I'm sure he's just making sure everyone is having a good time." I tried brushing off their words.

They all continued to stare at me in a placating way.

Bridget spoke up. "If you say so."

I quickly changed the topic. "So, are there munches held very often?"

Thankfully, they let the previous topic go. "We have a munch at The Local Cue on the first Friday of every month."

"The Local Cue?" I asked Priss, I think her name was.

"It's a billiards club over on Hamilton Street."

Bridget chimed in. "You should totally come next week."

We continued talking for the next hour or so. I learned so much listening to them talk about their lifestyle. It was fascinating. Soon though, the potluck was winding down, and I needed to get going.

"Thank you all for making me feel welcome. I debating getting out of my car for over thirty minutes, and I'm so glad I did. This was fun. I'm definitely going to come on Friday."

Bridget stood when I did, and I was surprised when she pulled me into a hug.

"It was so nice to meet you. I really do hope you'll come this weekend. We have so much fun and there are a ton of people I can introduce you to. We're an open and accepting group. Let me give you my phone number. If you ever have any questions about anything or just want someone to talk to, give me a call."

We exchanged phone numbers and I waved goodbye to everyone. I hadn't made it five feet before a sinful voice stopped me.

"Have you discovered any deep, dark secrets yet?" Marcus asked.

"Yours or mine?" I slowly turned to face him.

Marcus stepped closer and closer, edging me backward until I was flush with the wall behind me. The wall where this day began. He stopped just short of touching me. Instead, he leaned down, his warm breath caressing my ear.

"Why, yours, of course. I'm curious to know what depraved secrets you keep buried that you wish someone like me would discover. In fact, I think I would enjoy that immensely. Discovering your secrets, that is. Secrets I'm going to bet involve all the scandalous things you've fantasized about. A man binding your hands above your head while he feasts on your your sweet, succulent cunt."

I whimpered at the picture he painted, and my knees almost gave out. He was right. I did have those fantasies. I had to brace myself against the cement at my back.

He continued when he sensed my arousal. "You want to be fucked harder than you've ever been fucked before. Your ass spanked. You want to come like you've never come before."

Every scene flashed through my mind and god did I want it. I wanted everything he described. It terrified me this ecstasy flowing through me. I didn't even know this man, but I had a feeling that if, given the chance, he'd discover all my secrets.

Overwhelmed by the onslaught, I gasped. "I have to go."

Start the best-selling series today with SUBMISSION.
FREE with Kindle Unlimited!
Amazon: https://amzn.to/2WeWvHv

ACKNOWLEDGMENTS

I say this with every single book I write, yet I still haven't learned. I need to write down all the people who I need to acknowledge, because nothing about writing a book is done alone. From the person you message late at night crying because you can't figure out a plot point, to the authors who cheer you on every step of the way. There are so many people to be thankful for, and I'll do my best to include all of them.

Thank you to my amazing author friends who constantly listen to me bitch, moan, and whine. They also encourage me and push me. Thank you to the amazing Julia Sykes, Autumn Jones Lake, Murphy Wallace, TL Mayhew, Kellie Coakley, and all the authors in the Virtual Office and the Write 10K in a Day Challenge groups.

Thank you to my fantastic editor, Dayna Hart. You deal with my constant inability to hit a deadline and your insight and suggestions always make me think.

Thank you to my writing coach, Lauren Clarke, at Creating Ink. You've taught me so much about craft over these last few months.

Thank you to my alpha readers, Kathryn Parson and Antje Cartaxo.

Thank you to all the bloggers and bookstagrammers who shared Atonement with their readers! I appreciate all the hard work you guys do to run your blogs and pages.

Thank you to all the readers I've met both online and in person. I'm so thankful for all your support over the years. Thank you for loving my stories and sharing them with your friends. You are all absolutely amazing, and I couldn't do this without you!

Much love,
LK

Doms of Club Eden
Submission
Desire
Redemption
Protect
Betrayal
My Christmas Dom
Absolution
Forever (A prequel) - Coming July 2020

Love Undercover Series
In Too Deep
Striking Distance
Atonement

Other Books
Love Notes: A Dark Romance
SEALs in Love
Say Yes
Black Light: Possession
Saving Evie: A Brotherhood Protectors

LK Shaw resides in South Carolina with her high mainte-nance beagle mix dog, Miss P. An avid reader since child-hood, she became hooked on historical romance novels in high school. She now reads, and loves, all romance sub-genres, with dark romance and romantic suspense being her favorite. LK enjoys traveling and chocolate. Her books feature hot alpha heroes and the strong women they love.

LK also writes clean and sweet romance under the pseu-donym, Lily Prescott.

Want a FREE short story? Be sure to sign up for my news-letter and download your copy of A Birthday Spanking, a Doms of Club Eden prequel!
http://bit.ly/LKShawNewsletter

LK loves to interact with readers. You can follow her on any of her social media:

LK Shaw's Club Eden: https://www.facebook.com/groups/LKShawsClubEden
Author Page: www.facebook.com/LKShawAuthor
Author Profile: www.facebook.com/AuthorLKShaw
IG: @LKShaw_Author
Amazon: www.amazon.com/author/lkshaw
Bookbub: https://www.bookbub.com/authors/lk-shaw
Website: www.lkshawauthor.com